The girl gave a shrug and a little wry grimace. "Is it not a strange mystery that Apollon Zamp, the most zestful bravo of the showboats, plies the most cautious trade routes?"

"No strange mystery whatever! I am gallant and zestful because circumstances permit these qualities; otherwise I might be dull as a Ratwick clamdigger. I will tell you my secret. I make no demands upon my good friend Destiny. I never put him to the test, and hence we stride happily in step together through life."

"Perhaps your good friend Destiny is merely too polite to differ with you. Let us test his real opinion. Notice my talisman: one side bears my birth-sign, the other depicts the nymph Korakis. I will toss the talisman. If Korakis appears we sail on, past Badburg, up to Glassblower's Point. If not, Badburg."

She spun the ivory disk into the air; it fell to the table, rolled across the waxed wood to lean on edge against the wine flask.

Zamp looked down in annoyance. "So then—what am I to understand from this?"

"You would know better than I: you who walk arm in arm, like a brother, with Destiny."

"We walk together," said Apollon Zamp, "but we do not necessarily confide in each other. . . ."

"[Vance] can be exciting, satirical, funny, stark, tender, serious and thoughtful, all in the same story."

—Poul Anderson

Also by Jack Vance
Published by Tor Books

Araminta Station
Big Planet
Green Magic
The Languages of Pao

JACK VANCE
SHOWBOAT WORLD

A TOM DOHERTY ASSOCIATES BOOK
NEW YORK

The characters and situations in this book are entirely imaginary and bear no relation to any real person or actual happening.

SHOWBOAT WORLD

Copyright © 1975 by Jack Vance

A TOR Book
Published by Tom Doherty Associates, Inc.
49 West 24 Street
New York, N.Y. 10010

Cover art by Rodney Matthews

ISBN: 0-812-50093-8   Can. ISBN: 0-812-50092-X

Library of Congress Catalog Card Number: 75-554

First TOR edition: September 1989

Printed in the United States of America

0 9 8 7 6 5 4 3 2 1

SHOWBOAT WORLD

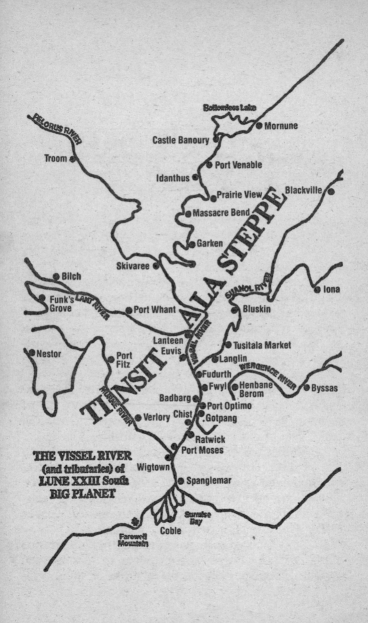

THE VISSEL RIVER
(and tributaries) of
LUNE XXIII South
BIG PLANET

From Handbook of the Inhabited Worlds:

Big Planet: the innermost planet of the yellow star Phaedra, a world 25,000 miles in diameter with a mean density slightly less than 2 and a surface gravity slightly in excess of Earth Standard.

The core of Big Planet, a glassy coalescence of calcium, silicon, aluminum, carbon, boron and various oxides, seems to have cooled and formed a crust, and later accumulated by accretion from space the present surface layers, which, like the core, are notably deficient in heavy elements. It may be noted that the three outer planets of the system are all extremely dense.

The surface of Big Planet is approximately half land and half water; the climate is generally similar to that of Earth. . . . Deposits of metal ore are almost nonexistent; metal of any sort is rare and valuable.

Big Planet lies beyond the frontier of terrestrial law, and has been settled by groups impatient with restraint, or determined to live by unorthodox tenets of conduct: nonconformists, anarchists, fugitives, religious dissidents, misanthropes, deviants, freaks. The tremendous expanses of Big Planet indifferently absorb them all.

In a few isolated districts something like civilization exists, though always in some more or less unusual variant. Elsewhere, beyond the environs of small communities, law is only as strong as local custom, or, as often, nonexistent. . . . The habits of life are infinitely varied, as over the centuries the heterogeneous groups, isolated and inbred, have diversified to florid extremes.

The savants of Earth have long pondered and analyzed and argued the circumstances of Big Planet. A hundred zealots have urged the imposition of terrestrial discipline, that law and order be brought to Big Planet, but those who defend the status quo have always had the final pronouncement: "Big Planet represents for us that tantalizing vision of the land beyond the frontier where bravery, resource and daring are more important than mastery of urban abstractions. The original settlers made great sacrifices to win freedom for themselves. In the process they willy-nilly determined the destiny of their descendants, so now the new generations share the idiosyncracies of the old, or indeed extend them to new limits. Who can deem this good or bad? Who can define justice or correctness or truth? If law is brought to Big Planet, if this glorious diversity is stifled, the dissidents are once again disenfranchised; once again they must move on, to havens even more remote. Big Planet is a wild world, and many dark deeds are done, but enforced uniformity only transfers the dilemma elsewhere. Big Planet in essence is a problem to which there exists no general solution.

Chapter 1

Where the river Vissel entered Surmise Bay stood Coble, a port for both sea-cogs and river barges, and terminus for the famous showboats of the region, such as *Fironzelle's Golden Conceit,* the *Pamellissa*, the *Melodious Hour, Miraldra's Enchantment*, the *Fireglass Prism*, the *Two Varminies*, and others of equal repute.

Up and down the Vissel roamed the showboats, as far north as Glassblower's Point or farther: to Skivaree or even Garken. The proprietors of the showboats, by the very nature of their trade, were a special sort, distinguished by vanity, avarice, and a peculiar sort of crafty resource difficult to define except in terms of deeds. Such qualities aside, these men differed sharply. Lemuriel Boke wore striped garments of black, red and brown, and adorned his head with the triple-tiered bonnet of an Ultimate Pantologist; he blanched his skin stark white and spoke in a cellar-deep voice. Umber Stroon was as effusive as Boke was saturnine. He used terms of grandiloquent vainglory in connection with himself and equally striking figures of disparagement in regard to his competitors. Darik Dankzy carried a rapier and a brace of snapples in his sash and was quick to rebuff all discourtesies, while Garth Ashgale affected an elegant languor. Eleusis Munt wore vests and pantaloons of perfumed silk; his language was rich in sentiment and the fervor of his nature flowed forth in love for man, woman and child alike, sometimes to embarrassing excess. Fring the Fantast was shrewd, patient and frugal; Apollon Zamp swaggered his decks like a hero of legend and spent as fast as he earned; and so it went along the Vissel.

As for the showboats themselves, *Fironzelle's Golden Conceit* and *Miraldra's Enchantment* were reckoned the finest, and the rivalry between the shipmasters, Garth Ashgale and Apollon Zamp respectively, was of long standing. Zamp's entertainments were characterized by brisk pace, flair, sudden shocks and impacts; he emphasized farce, mummery, prestidigitation, eccentric dances and reenactments of notorious atrocities. Garth Ashgale preferred to present extravaganzas rather more leisurely and elaborate. Zamp, in spite of his casual and swaggering semblance, was an exacting taskmaster who demanded both virtuosity and versatility from his troupe, whereas Ashgale built his spectacles upon the talents of proved specialists. Zamp's productions were supple and vivacious; Ashgale specialized in tragic drama: *Emphyrio; Lucas and Portmena; The Blue Pomegranate; The Reign of the Iron King*. Ashgale's costumes were sumptuous; his sets fascinated the eye; his dedication to verisimilitude, notably in scenes of erotic ardor and the imposition of justice, far transcended the efforts of those who sought to satisfy their customers with simulations and offstage outcries.

Ashgale ranged far and wide, up the Vissel to Lanteen and beyond, out along tributaries such as the Suanol, the Wergence, the Murne. Zamp preferred to play the towns of the Lower Vissel, with an occasional sortie up the Murne, where the prejudices of the people were familiar and their commodities* of known value.

On one occasion while the boat lay at anchor off the town Ratwick, a red-haired mime-girl twitted him for his discretion. "Poof!" she said, giving his trim blond goatee a tug. "Must we prowl the same old shores forever? Up, down, up, down, from Thamet to Wigtown to Badburg, and only a pause at Coble to iron† your money."

Zamp laughed without rancor, and drained his goblet of wine; the two had just taken a meal in Zamp's stern cabin. "And if by this means I dine on the best with a charming companion, why should I change?"

The girl, who called herself Lael-Rosza, gave a shrug and a little wry grimace. "Do you really want reasons?"

"Naturally! If reasons exist!"

"There are no reasons, except to see different faces and different scenery. But is it not a strange mystery that Apollon Zamp, the most zestful bravo of the showboats, plies the most cautious routes?"

"No strange mystery whatever! I am gallant and zestful because circumstances permit these qualities; otherwise I might be as dull as a Ratwick clamdigger. I will tell you my secret." Zamp made a significant gesture and leaned forward. "I make no demands upon my good friend Destiny. I never put him to the test, and hence we stride happily in step together through life."

"Perhaps your good friend Destiny is merely too modest and too polite to differ with you," suggested

---

*The basic standard of value everywhere across Big Planet is iron, the least scarce of the metals. An iron groat—to the mass of about half a gram—represents the ordinary wage for a day of common toil.

†Colloquialism: the process of exchanging miscellaneous tokens, gems and commodities into iron.

Lael-Rosza. "Let us test his real opinion. Ahead of us is Badburg, that dreary little group of hovels where the folk pay their way in pickled fish. Notice my talisman: one side bears my birth-sign, the other depicts the nymph Korakis. I will toss up the talisman. If Korakis appears we sail on, past Badburg, up to Fudurth, or Euvis, or even Lanteen at Glassblower's Point. If not, Badburg. Do you agree?"

Zamp shook his head. "Destiny admittedly has his little quirks; for instance he never troubles to control the twirl of a talisman."

"Still, I will twirl." Lael-Rosza spun the ivory disk into the air; it fell to the table, rolled across the waxed wood to lean on edge against the wine flask.

Zamp looked down in annoyance. "So then—what am I expected to understand from this?"

"You must ask someone else; I have no skill with omens."

Zamp raised his eyebrows. "Omens?"

"You would know better than I: you who walk arm in arm, like a brother, with Destiny."

"We walk together," said Apollon Zamp, "but we do not necessarily confide in each other."

The night was well advanced. Lael-Rosza had slipped quietly back to her cubicle on the deck below, and Apollon Zamp, who had taken perhaps a draught or two more than necessary, sat back in his massive chair of carved pfalax wood. The night was warm; the casements were open; a breeze caused the flame in the lamps to flicker, and shadows danced around the walls. Zamp rose to his feet and surveyed the cabin: a chamber which any man might envy, with furniture of massive pfalax, a cabinet of glass flagons twinkling in the lamplight, a good bed with a green coverlet in the alcove.

The tamarack knees supporting the overhead beams were carved in scrolls; the oak deck below his feet shone dark and glossy with wax, one great lamp hung above the table, another over the desk. At this late hour the various levels of Zamp's mind lay open to each other. Images surged and spun; portents and meanings were everywhere if only he were clever enough to grasp them. The casements reflected a distorted semblance of himself. Zamp peered close to see a recognizable person, one dear and familiar, yet somehow awful and strange and remote. The figure was squat, with bulging buttocks, garments hanging all askew. The fair curls flapped foppishly long; blue eyes looked vacuously past a long, pale nose. Zamp straightened himself in indignation; the creature in the casement blinked and rippled and stared back with an indignant life of its own, as if it found Zamp's appearance as revolting as Zamp found its own. . . . Zamp turned away. If these were presages or messages, or insights, he wanted no more of them.

He stepped out into the night and climbed to the quarterdeck. The dark stream slid past without haste, aware that its course was inexorable. From Ratwick a few late lamps glimmered yellow on the water.

Zamp looked about the vessel with automatic vigilance. All seemed in order. He went to lean on the taffrail. In the light from the stern lantern he noted on the bulge of the rudder a small squat bulwig, the lamplight reflecting stars in its three eyes. Zamp and the bulwig stared at each other. Zamp willed the creature to jump into the water. It hunched itself down more obdurately than ever. Zamp projected the full force of his personality. "Go!" he muttered. "Depart from the rudder, mud-scut! Back to the slime!"

The bulwig's gaze seemed to become more intense, and it occurred to Zamp that the bulwig in its turn might be willing Zamp back from the rail. "Bah," muttered Zamp. "What nonsense! I am turning away only because I have business elsewhere!"

On his way below he paused to consider Ratwick once more. Today he had presented a farce, *The Drunken Fishmonger and the Talking Eel*, together with a "Ballet of the Flowers," featuring his eight mime-girls in flounced robes; a wrestling match between the ship's professional and the local champion; and a finale which included the eight girls, the orchestra, two jugglers, three sword dancers and six grotesques. The program had been carefully adapted to the prejudices of the town, which like most communities of Big Planet considered itself the single oasis of sanity upon all the vast surface of the planet. He had played to three hundred and twelve men, women and children; he had collected in payment over four thousand ounces of driftwood resin, convertible at Coble—so Zamp had determined from his *Transactional Bulletin*—into ninety-five groats of iron. A fair day's take, neither good nor bad. Tomorrow he had planned to hoist anchor and drift back down-river, and why not? What was up-river save a few dingy little villages too poor even to tempt the robber nomads from Tinsitala Steppe? Lanteen at Glassblower's Point was prosperous enough, and his own few visits had yielded adequate returns. He was growing no younger. . . . Odd! What had propelled that totally irrelevant idea into his mind? He turned one last thoughtful look around the river, then descended to his cabin and went to bed.

Chapter 2

Zamp awoke to find the light of Phaedra slanting across the oak planks of the cabin floor. Water chuckled under the stern as wind from the south worked up a chop against the current, and with the anchor rode slack the vessel moved restlessly from side to side. Zamp stretched and groaned, climbed from bed, pulled the bell-cord for his breakfast, and arrayed himself in his morning robe.

Chaunt the steward laid the great pfalax table with a white cloth, poured a bowl of tea, arranged a basket of fruit to hand, then served a ragout of reed-birds in a crusty shell.

Zamp ate a leisurely and pensive breakfast, then called for Bonko the boatswain, a burly, big-bellied man with long arms and short legs and a bony head, bald except for bristling black eyebrows and a small moustache under his splayed lump of a nose. Bonko's demeanor, which was courteous and accommodating, belied his appearance. In addition to his navigational offices, he served as ship's wrestler and executioner in those dramas which specified such a role.

"How goes the day?" asked Zamp.

"The south wind is brisk and dead in our teeth. We'll

make no progress down-river unless we use the animals, which means the towpath."

Zamp gave his head a shake of displeasure. "The towpath south of Ratwick is a quagmire. Has Quaner finished with the drive axle?"

"No, sir, it's still out for glazing and he feels that the gland must be repacked."

Last night the talisman, rolling across the table, had come to rest on its edge! "Very well," said Zamp. "Up all sails! If we can't go south, we'll lay hold of this fine wind for the north. We haven't played Euvis or Fudurth or Port Fitz for years."

"I seem to recall some small trouble at Port Fitz," said Bonko cautiously, "in connection with a lady wearing antlers."

Zamp grunted. "The customs of these wretched folk are far too unyielding. Still, I don't care to desecrate another of their totems. Euvis may be as far north as we care to venture. Up all sails; raise the anchor."

Bonko went forward to order out the deck gang. A few minutes later Zamp heard the creak of blocks and a clicking of the capstan, and the great vessel came alive to the pressure of the wind.

Zamp went up to the quarterdeck and watched Ratwick fall astern. At this point the Vissel River flowed wide and free, with the western shore an all but invisible smudge. In the sunlight and wind, Zamp's qualms and eerie introspections of the night before evaporated; the occasion seemed as remote as a dream. The single and only verity was *now*, with wind blowing the reek of water and mud, wet reeds, dingle and black-willow into his face, and the sunlight dancing upon the water. The yards had been braced; the mainsail and foresail billowed and strained, and Bonko was setting out the sky-master. The ship surged majestically through the water. A delightful privilege to be alive, thought Zamp—especially in the guise and substance of himself, the noblest and best of the Vissel impresarios! Garth Ashgale? Of no more consequence than yonder gape-mouthed fisherman huddling in his scow as *Miraldra's Enchantment* surged past. Zamp raised his arm in an expansive salute. Who knows? Next time past the fisherman would remember the magnificent ship with its gallant captain and bring himself and his bit of iron aboard for a performance. The fisherman gave no answering signal and merely stared back numbly. Zamp lowered his arm. Such a lumpkin would be just as likely to blunder aboard *Fironzelle's Golden Conceit* should that bargeload of sham drift past. Ashgale had sailed forth in his gaudy palace two weeks before Zamp's own departure from Coble, and they had passed nowhere along the river. Ah, well, Ashgale could come and go as he wished, his acts meant nothing and Zamp went forward to make an inspection of the boat.

Zamp's gait was most distinctive. His torso was sturdy, although good living had blurred the taut outline of his middle regions. His legs were long; he walked with a loping bent-kneed stride, shoulders hunched, head somewhat forward, with blue eyes gleaming, fair hair flouncing and aristocratic nose turned first to this side, then that.

On the midship platform the acrobats and jugglers were at practice, with the animal-trainers and insectmasters under screened awnings to port and starboard. On the foredeck the mime troupe rehearsed their routines, quarreling for space with the grotesques who attempted a new contortion. On the stage itself the Dildeks, who simulated combat with knives, bolos, claws and snapples, ran back and forth across chalked patterns.

Zamp climbed the shrouds to the crow's nest, but observed no cushions, bottles, musical instruments or undergarments, all of which he had discovered at one time or another. The eye at the end line of the triatic stay joining foremast and mainmast showed evidence of chafe. This was the high-wire upon which his funambulists performed their feats. If it broke during a performance, Zamp's professional reputation would suffer; he would have a word with Bonko at once.

From this lofty perch the boat presented a scene of cheerful activity; everyone seemed in good spirits. Zamp knew better. *Miraldra's Enchantment* carried its full quota of dyspeptic grumblers. Some told of idyllic conditions aboard rival boats; others, slaves to avarice, incessantly demanded iron and more iron. Up here in the crow's nest, Zamp could ignore all that was paltry and take pleasure in the view, which extended forever across the vast Big Planet horizons. That far smudge was a line of mountains; that fainter air-colored mark beyond was another, higher, range; and still beyond, at the uncertain limits of perception, a silken line of pale blue ink or gray paper represented still another mountain range of unknown proportions. A glint in the west might be a sea, and that trace of smoky lavender along the far shore perhaps indicated a desert. Southward the brimming river dwindled to a twinkling thread of silver; to the north a sugarloaf bluff of red chert concealed the course of the river across the Tinsitala Steppe, onward and onward: where? Past Badburg and Fudurth, and Glassblower's Point; past the Meagh Mountains and Dead Horse Swamp and Garken; across Slyland, through the Mandaman Gates into Bottomless Lake and the legendary kingdom of Soyvanesse, whose people lived in mansions and dined off iron plates and allowed no strangers to enter, in order to protect their wealth and the suavity of their lives. The *River Index* showed these places, but who knows? The chart might be factitious. Zamp knew of folk who had journeyed north as far as Garken, but the lands beyond were no more real than the marks on the chart. Zamp nodded his head sagely. So much for the worlds of fancy! Reality lay here, along the Vissel, from Coble to Ratwick, or perhaps Euvis; here was real iron, and a pinch of black in the hand was worth more than clangorous disks and noble bowls of the imagination.

Zamp descended the shrouds and strode back to the quarterdeck, where he flung himself into a wicker chair and sat staring moodily across the water.

At noon the wind slackened and the ship moved upstream only listlessly, barely making way against the current, and Zamp was forced to anchor overnight in midstream.

In the morning the monsoon again blew steady and set the boat plunging through the water. At noon the lookout spied Gotpang Bump on the horizon, and presently Gotpang Town: a crusty efflorescence of stone huts up the steep stone sides of the Bump. A stone wall around the summit enclosed a stone cloister half-hidden in an ancient orchard of madura orange trees. Here was housed that fraternity of cenobites known as the Actuarians, who fixed the local terms of birth and death. Zamp had played Gotpang ten years previously to no great financial advantage, and since had passed it by. Today he had the choice of putting into Gotpang and performing possibly for small profit, or anchoring again in midstream with no profit whatever. Zamp decided to stop at Gotpang.

He refreshed his memory from the *River Index* and was advised to make no reference to disease, accident or death, nor to suggest that birth could be achieved other than through the cooperation of an Actuarian.

At the base of the Bump a jetty enclosed a snug little harbor; the flat to the back provided space for a pair of warehouses, three taverns and a small marketplace. Already at the dock, to Zamp's annoyance, was the *Two Varminies*, operated by a certain Osso Santelmus, who presented what Zamp considered a rather paltry program of slapstick farce, animal acts and a minstrel who sang ballads to the accompaniment of a guitar. Santelmus augmented his income with games of chance, the sale of tonics, lotions and salves, and a booth where he foretold the future.

Zamp glumly ordered *Miraldra's Enchantment* to the dock. Neither boat would destroy the custom of the other; indeed, a pair of boats in competition often augmented trade for both. Zamp felt assured that such would not be the case at Gotpang.

As soon as his boat was secure, Zamp, as etiquette demanded, went aboard the *Two Varminies* to pay his respects to Osso Santelmus. The two sat down to a bottle of brandy in the after cabin.

Santelmus had nothing good to remark about either Gotpang or the Actuarians. "Every year they impose three new ordinances. I learn now that I cannot advertise my Miracle Bath as a sure elixir of charm and beauty, nor may I foretell the future unless I first obtain an approved forecast from the Bureau of Schedules."

Zamp shook his head in disgust. "Petty officials are always anxious to justify their existences."

"True. Nonetheless, I mute my complaints. Experience has taught me the defense against pettifoggery. I now offer my Miracle Bath only as a soothing lotion, with mildly laxative qualities if taken internally. In my booth I command voices of the dead, and I achieve approximately equal earnings. But let us speak of a more elevating subject. How do you rate your chances at Mornune?"

Zamp stared, blue eyes wide in wonder. "My chances where?"

Santelmus poured more brandy. "Come now, my friend; between the two of us evasiveness surely is out of order. I too am bound for Lanteen, but I doubt if my entertainments, diverting though they may be, will enthrall King Waldemar's emissary. The choice, I suspect, lies between yourself and Garth Ashgale."

Zamp said, "I have no idea of what you are talking about."

Now it was Santelmus's turn to star in wonder. "Surely you received notice of the great occasion? It was announced at the Coble conclave not a month ago!"

"I did not attend the conclave."

"True! Now I recall as much. Garth Ashgale volunteered to convey the information to you."

Zamp set his goblet down with a thump. "Just as the vulp* in the fable volunteered to notify the farmer of the break in the fowl-yard fence."

"Aha," said Santelmus, "Ashgale evidently failed to bring you the news?"

"All I saw of Ashgale was the stern of his boat moving full-speed up the river."

Santelmus gave his head a doleful shake, as if the scope of human iniquity were a never-ending source of wonder. "The news is simple but startling. You know of King Waldemar and the realm Soyvanesse beyond the Bottomless Lake?"

---

*Vulp: a small voracious predator, common throughout the Dalkenberg region of south-central Lune XXIII.

Zamp made a noncommittal gesture. "We are hardly personal friends."

"King Waldemar is new on the throne, but already famous for splendid impulses. His latest concept is a Grand Festival at Mornune, and he has ordained a competition between the entertainment troupes of all the Dalkenberg, from north, east, south and west of Bottomless Lake. The news which pertains to us is this: at Lanteen, one week from today, an adjudicator will select a showboat to represent the Lower Vissel at the festival."

"Indeed! And the grand prize?"

"The leader of the victorious troupe will receive a patent of nobility, a palace at Mornune, and a treasure of metal: enough to excite even a tired old charlatan like myself!"

"Do not belittle your very real talents! But was it not a naïve act to entrust my notification to Garth Ashgale?"

"So it now would appear," said Santelmus, pulling at his chin. "At the time there was much expansive talk; some said this and some said that. Garth Ashgale remarked, 'Imagine the excitement of our colleague Apollon Zamp when he learns of this rich competition! Why not allow me to surprise him with the news?' Everyone agreed to the suggestion, and Garth Ashgale departed, presumably to seek you out."

"He will find me at Lanteen," said Zamp.

Santelmus heaved a sigh. "So now it is definite. You have decided to compete for the great prize at Mornune."

Zamp held up his hand in a gesture of disclaimer. "Not so fast! Mornune lies at the far edge of a wilderness; why tempt the certain attention of the Tinsitala robbers?"

Santelmus gave an unctuous chuckle. "And you are anxious that Garth Ashgale be spared these same dangers?"

Zamp drained his cup and set it deliberately down upon the table. "All of us have played a prank or two in our time; nonetheless, I absolutely deplore the self-serving turpitude which Garth Ashgale has so vividly demonstrated. I intend to refute it."

"In principle I also deplore turpitude," said Santelmus. He lifted the jug. "I see no reason why we should not take another drop or two to certify this proposition."

"Nor I."

Chapter 3

From Gotpang the Vissel swung back and forth in lazy loops across the Sarklentine Swamp. Purple and lavender fern-trees hung over the water with clusters of spore pods pendent from the frond-tips. Channels and sloughs slanted away to invisibility behind islands of green and black reeds; everywhere flew flocks of black-birds*; coots and loons fluttered along the surface of the water. The wind, while fitful, never failed completely, to Zamp's relief, for the swamp allowed no towpaths and Ship's Engineer Elias Quaner had not yet repaired the linkage between drive-capstans and the propeller shaft.

Quietly up the river floated *Miraldra's Enchantment*, leaving a barely perceptible wake, no more than a turbulence of brown water. Zamp worked in his cabin adapting a complicated old musical farce to the talents of his company. At dusk the boat tied up to the rotting wharf of a long-deserted hamlet. Three young acrobats went exploring the pallid ghost-huts and came upon a

---

*No avians are indigenous to Big Planet. Birds and fowl are all immigrants from Earth, as are many varieties of vegetation. Most undergo a swift evolutionary transition to new types.

rare swamp-oel* which ran clicking after them along the dock. Zamp attempted to capture the valuable creature with a cargo net, but it emitted a horrid stench and fled through the reeds.

The night passed quietly under a blaze of stars; dawn came cool and calm and Phaedra rose into cloudless sky.

Zamp climbed to the crow's nest and looked for signs of wind; he saw only vast expanses of reeds, an occasional rotting hag-tree, and the motionless surface of the river.

An hour later Elias Quarner† reported that the capstan drive might now be used. Zamp at once ordered up the ship's complement of bullocks, which were harnessed to the staves of the capstans and set to toiling around and around a twenty-foot circle. Water roiled behind the propeller; the ship moved forward. Halfway through the morning the south wind arrived. The sails billowed taut and thrust the boat northward.

A line of low hills approached the river; at the base huddled the town Port Optimo. For reasons best known to themselves the citizens of the town spoke a secret gibberish and pretended not to comprehend standard speech. From time to time Zamp played a program at Port Optimo, earning no great profit, for when he tried to haggle with the folk of the town over the price of the commodities with which they paid their admissions,

---

*Oel: a creature indigenous to Big Planet and found in many varieties. Typically the creature stands seven feet tall on two short legs, with a narrow four-horned head of twisted cartilage. Its black dorsal carapace hangs low to the ground; to its ventral surface are folded a dozen clawed arms. From a distance an oel might be mistaken for a gigantic beetle running on its hind legs.

†The Quaners: a caste of engineers, architects and builders, active everywhere across the Dalkenberg.

they were never able to understand his remarks. Today, with the wind blowing fresh and fair, Zamp decided to press onward.

On the following day the boat passed the towns Badburg and Fwyl, and late in the afternoon put into Fudurth, where the Suanol joined the Vissel. Fudurth, ordinarily Zamp's northernmost port of call, had originally been established by traders as a transshipment point for goods and wares brought down the Suanol from the Barthelmian Uplands and the town's lack of special quirks was almost a peculiarity in itself.

Zamp presented his program to a full house, which gave the new musical farce a cordial reception.

In the morning Zamp once more set sail to the north, and all day fared across a flat dismal land, barren except for furze and garnet-bush, and at sunset the blue-gray outline of Glassblower's Point, at the confluence of the Lant with the Vissel, rose against the horizon. Nomads shunned this particular area and Zamp felt safe passing the night moored to a gnarled spatterack on the western shore.

All next day the winds teased Zamp, puffing and dying, slanting and veering and backing the sails, and Zamp thought to spend another night on the river, but late in the afternoon the wind steadied and blew fair. Zamp ordered up the sky-master and the great bluff bow crumpled and crushed the surface of the river to pale foam.

At sunset the wind slackened to a whisper, barely sufficient to hold the boat steady against the current, with Glassblower's Point and Lanteen still seven miles distant. Zamp, now irritated at the elements, ordered bullocks to the capstans. *Miraldra's Enchantment* moved forward once more, riding water glossy as silk.

Zamp hugged the western shore to avoid the weight

of the Lant current. Glassblower's Point loomed overhead, with the lamps of Lanteen glimmering on its far
flank. Zamp brought the boat even closer to the shore
and riding an eddy from the Lant, nosed quietly up to
the Lanteen dock, and moored directly astern of
Fironzelle's Golden Conceit.

Ashgale's cabin showed no light, and indeed the
entire ship was dark, except for the masthead beacon
and a set of thief-lamps along the rails.

As soon as hawsers had been set out, Zamp retired to
his cabin where he donned one of his most splendid
outfits: pale blue breeches, puffed and tucked at the
knees, a black high-shouldered coat, a white shirt clasped
at wrist and neck with buckles of iron-skin. From his
locker he brought a fine blue hat which he brushed and
laid aside. Into his sash he thrust a dress rapier; into his
coat he tucked a kerchief and a small pomander. He
combed out his fair curls, clipped a few strands from
his goatee, clapped the hat on his head and marched
ashore.

Etiquette required that he pay a call to Garth Ashgale
aboard his ship, a duty which Zamp would have will
ingly neglected, but why provoke the sneers of his
rival? Decorum, after all, was a more subtle and ultimately more satisfactory weapon than high feelings and
improper conduct.

He mounted the gangplank to *Fironzelle's Golden
Conceit*, and halting on the deck looked right and left.
The gangway watchman sat by the felon's cage con-
versing with a prisoner. All else aboard was quiet.
Without haste or smartness the gangway watchman rose
to his feet and ambled toward Zamp, who waited with
raised eyebrows at the lack of punctilio. Aboard
Miraldra's Enchantment affairs went differently.

The watchman recognized Zamp, and touched his

forehead. "Good evening to you, sir. I fear that Master Ashgale is off somewhere ashore; in fact I would be willing to change places with him this very instant."

Zamp acknowledged the information with a curt nod. "Have you knowledge of where he might be found?"

"I can provide a reasonable guess. Five taverns replenish the good folk of this town, of which The Jolly Glassblower is the most select. At this location, by all tenets of logic, Master Ashgale should be found."

Zamp looked around the vessel. "Master Ashgale has been giving daily performances?"

"This is the case, and I have never known him to be so meticulous in regard to detail. The productions have aroused favorable comment."

From the cage came a call: "Jailer, what is the hour of the night?"

The watchman called back: "Why trouble to ask? You are going nowhere." He winked at Zamp. "What do you think of this great hulk of bloodthirsty mischief? Master Ashgale gave ten groats of iron for him. The Lanteeners are religiously inclined and not allowed the pleasure of cutting his throat."

Zamp, peering into the cage, saw a black-bearded face and a pair of glittering eyes "Impressive. What was his crime?"

"Brigandage, raid, atrocity and murder. Still, all in all, not so bad a fellow."

"Where then is my beer?" the prisoner called out.

"All in good time," replied the watchman.

Zamp asked: "Master Ashgale evidently has scheduled a tragic drama?"

"We are to play *Emphyrio* presently, perhaps for the competition. The prisoner refuses to learn his lines, surly fellow that he is. Still, in his place I might take no great interest in the production either."

"Jailer!" called the prisoner. "I am ready to take my beer!"

"In due course. Have you memorized the speech?"

"Yes, yes," grumbled the prisoner. "Must I recite to you?"

"These were Master Ashgale's instructions."

In a bored voice the prisoner declaimed, " 'Prince Orchelstyne, how you have betrayed me! Forever will shame shroud your name! Never will you know the love of Rusemund, though you come to her splendid in pearls and iron! My ghost, dank and terrible, will stand between when you seek to enclasp her! Take my life then, Prince Orchelstyne'—I forget the rest."

"Hmm," said the watchman. "Your style is far from convincing. Still, who am I to deny you your beer?"

"Good evening to you both," said Zamp and descended the gangway. He walked up the esplanade, where flaring orange torches illuminated booths selling fried whitebait, mounded pink sweetmeats, skewers of barbecued clams. Farther along the dock loomed the hulls of several other showboats which Zamp could not surely identify; the nearest, he thought to be Lemuriel Boke's *Chrysanthe*.

A sign hanging over the esplanade identified The Jolly Glassblower, a structure of brown glass brick and weathered timber. Zamp entered, to find himself in a great room lit by twenty lamps of red, blue and green glass. Benches, tables and booths were crowded with townspeople in knee-length smocks and low flat-crowned hats, as well as folk from the showboats. The air was warm and heavy with the sound of voices, laughter, the clink of goblets, a thin, wailing music. Lamplight sparkled and refracted from a thousand glass baubles and oddments. A side of beef turned on a spit beside a vertical bed of coals; a cook naked to the waist, sweating and shining in the fire-glow, basted the meat with sauce from a tray and carved to order of the patrons. On a platform at the far end of the room sat an orchestra of four nomads, wearing red and brown shag trousers, black leather vests, cocked hats of black felt. With concertina, screedle, thump-box and guitar they played a merry quickstep, to which a man more than half-drunk solemnly attempted a jig, with indifferent success.

Garth Ashgale sat in a booth to the side of the room: a handsome dark-haired man, grave and pale, several years older than Zamp, with an exquisite air of elegant self-assurance. Beside him sat a young woman of distinguished appearance. A long black cape hung at a dramatic slant from her shoulders; a soft black cap controlled glossy hair, as fair as Zamp's own, which fell artlessly to the line of her jaw. A young woman of considerable charm, thought Zamp, though her aristocratic hauteur appealed to him no more than did Garth Ashgale's languid sophistication.

Zamp shot his cuffs, set his coat to best advantage. He approached the booth, doffed his hat and performed a punctilious bow, and had the satisfaction of seeing Garth Ashgale's eyebrows rise. "Good evening to you, Master Ashgale."

"I wish you as well, Master Zamp." Ashgale made no effort to introduce the young woman, who gave Zamp a look of supercilious distaste, then turned her gaze toward the musicians.

"I am surprised to find you here," said Zamp. "At Coble, if you recall, we discussed the leak in your garboard strake, and a day or so later I was told that you had put into the Surmise Boatworks for repairs."

Garth Ashgale smilingly shook his head. "Some mendacious person has amused himself at your expense."

"This is quite possible," said Zamp. "I am a simple

man, and I have achieved my status through simple excellence. Others have used malice and machination against me, but what have they gained? Nothing. I ignore such folk, and if they now look after me and grind their teeth in envy, what do I care?''

"The point is well taken," declared Ashgale. "As for your reputation, it is justly deserved. Your trained insects are consistently amusing and I believe your grotesques to be the most repulsive anywhere along the river. Still—what brings you so far north, you who are so notoriously partial to the outskirts of Coble?''

Zamp made a placid sign. "No particular reason. A few months ago I declined King Waldemar's invitation to play the Mornune Festival and I suggested a set of trials to select a substitute. This is the course he adopted, and I am on hand to witness the occasion and to advise King Waldemar's representatives in regard to the worth of the competing ship masters.''

Garth Ashgale raised his eyes to the ceiling and shook his head wonderingly. Zamp meanwhile attracted the attention of a waiter. "I will have ale; also serve this charming lady and Master Ashgale according to their needs.''

The young woman gave an indifferent shrug. Garth Ashgale gestured to the empty wine bottle; the waiter hastened off to fulfill the order.

Zamp said, "Along the way I met Master Osso Santelmus, and I believe that several other boats of quality equal to the *Two Varminies* and *Fironzelle's Golden Conceit* are on the way. The trials will be amusing to watch.''

Garth Ashgale's easy smile had become strained. "So you will not compete?''

Zamp signified in the negative. "I have wealth, health and honor; what do I lack? Let others strive after elusive goals. But come, Garth Ashgale, where are your manners? Why do you not introduce me to your companion?''

Ashgale turned an amused glance toward the young woman. "Because I am not acquainted with her. The tavern was full; I asked if I might share her table and this she graciously allowed.''

The young woman rose to her feet. "You may now use the table in its entirety." With a cool inclination of her head she crossed the room and departed the tavern.

Zamp stared after the supple form. "What a peculiar person!''

" 'Peculiar'?" Garth Ashgale shrugged and raised his eyebrows, as if perplexed by the quality of Zamp's standards. "I thought her quite charming.''

"No dispute on this account," said Zamp. "But is she not an unusual person to find here at Lanteen? Surely she is not some glassblower's daughter?''

"I was on the point of making inquiry when you arrived," said Garth Ashgale, "and now I believe I will return to my ship. Good evening to you, Apollon Zamp.''

The two men exchanged salutes, and Garth Ashgale departed the tavern. Zamp immediately summoned the waiter. "The lady in the black cape who sat at this table: are you acquainted with her name?''

"No, sir. She has engaged a chamber at the Alderman's Hostel and regularly takes her meals with us. She conducts herself with the pride of a noblewoman and pays in good iron groats; otherwise nothing is known.''

"A rather mysterious person, in short.''

"So much might well be said, sir.''

Zamp sat for an hour, listening to the music and watching the glassblowers at their loose-kneed jigs.

Certain decisions must be made. By arriving at Lanteen

he had demonstrated to Ashgale the futility of his paltry deceptions; but now: should he proceed further and attempt to earn the invitation to Mornune? To succeed would be pleasant; to fail would be correspondingly bitter—even though Zamp felt no inclination whatever to undertake the long upstream voyage to the Bottomless Lake.

He made his decision. He would compete, but only as if in a careless, half-serious manner. His principal rival would of course be Garth Ashgale, and two methods of attaining victory suggested themselves. He could strain every nerve to produce an obviously superior entertainment, or he could use equal diligence to ensure the inferiority of Garth Ashgale's presentation. Both options must be explored from all angles.

Zamp mused a few moments longer, then paid his score and departed the tavern. The vendors along the esplanade were now darkening their lamps and wheeling away their booths. Mist blowing down from the north obscured the water and swirled around the masthead lamps of the docked vessels. Tomorrow no doubt would see the arrival of the *Two Varminies* and perhaps other boats, none of which need be seriously feared. *Fironzelle's Golden Conceit*, however, could not be dismissed so lightly. Garth Ashgale, for all his elegant ways and wicked duplicities, had achieved many notable successes; the fact could not be disputed.

In deep thought Zamp returned to his ship, noting, as he passed, the light in the stern cabin of *Fironzelle's Golden Conceit*, where Garth Ashgale no doubt sat preoccupied with his own calculations.

On the following day, as Zamp had expected, Osso Santelmus arrived with his *Two Varminies* followed one after the other, by the *Psychopompos Revenant* and the *Vissel Dominator*.

Santelmus came aboard *Miraldra's Enchantment* to take a glass of spirits and to exchange gossip with Zamp. "A very adequate turnout; I foresee intense competition ahead."

"Unquestionably," said Zamp. "But I still lack certain elements of information. For instance, when does this event occur? How will it be conducted? Who makes the judgments?"

"Had you received the initial announcement," said Santelmus, "you would not have needed to ask. We are merely to present ourselves here on this day, and further information will then be forthcoming. I suppose that you have been preparing a remarkable new production?"

"The time is too short," said Zamp. "I will simply play one of my musical farces."

"There will be no novelties aboard the *Two Varminies*," said Santelmus. "I do not expect to win unless the river swallows up all the other contestants, so why exert myself?"

Zamp refilled the glasses with brandy. "You are much too pessimistic."

Santelmus sadly shook his head. "My triumphs are all in the past. I recall that in order to demonstrate my Bath of Beauty I employed two sisters. I would call for a volunteer from the spectators and the ugly sister would step forward and enter the bath, where the beautiful sister already crouched. I would pour in a gill of my Rainbow Essence, and the beautiful sister would spring forth exultant. The stratagem earned considerable sums of iron."

"So why did you abandon it?"

"Circumstances compelled a change. The sisters became disgruntled, and one day they spitefully reversed their roles. I was helpless to prevent the beautiful girl from jumping into the bath, apparently to emerge long-nosed and pockmarked. The event unnerved me and I was never able to continue.''

''I have suffered similar embarrassments,'' said Zamp. ''At Langlin on the Suanol the sound of the letter 'r' is considered an offensive obscenity, and at my introductory speech I was pelted with stones which they had brought along for this purpose.''

''The artist's life is at least eventful.'' Santelmus rose to his feet. ''Well, I must see to my affairs.''

Walking out on deck the two were attracted by the sound of declamations and music from *Fironzelle's Golden Conceit*. Santelmus nodded sagely. ''Garth Ashgale is intent at his rehearsals; he is not one to ignore any detail. What is that pounding noise?''

''I don't know,'' said Zamp. ''No doubt a repair of some sort.''

Santelmus descended the gangplank and Zamp immediately clambered up into the crow's nest, where he could overlook the length of *Fironzelle's Golden Conceit*. It appeared that Ashgale, like Zamp, had been experiencing difficulty with his drive shaft. The great member of resin-treated skeel had been hoisted to the quarterdeck and laid out on trestles for scraping and justification. Zamp's own engineer, Elias Quaner, stood discussing the problem with his kinsman, the engineer aboard *Fironzelle's Golden Conceit*.

Zamp descended to the deck, and when Quaner returned summoned him to the stern cabin. ''How goes Ashgale's drive shaft?''

''Not too badly. A simple case of warp, which must be cured with steam and pressure.''

''And the propeller?''

''It has been taken to the boatyard for refinishing.

Master Ashgale intends a long voyage north, and insists that all be in best condition.''

Zamp brought out his best brandy and poured generously into a goblet which he handed to Elias Quaner. "No doubt you know why we are here?"

"I have heard rumors of a competition at Mornune."

"The rumors are accurate. Now, it goes without saying that if *Miraldra's Enchantment* prospers, all of us prosper."

Elias Quaner, a short man with earnest blue eyes and red-brown hair worn in the typical Quaner tufts, responded cautiously, "That would be the general hope."

Zamp developed his ideas a step further. "We can either exert ourselves to win, or ensure that Ashgale loses."

"Or both."

"As you say, both . . . Ashgale's drive shaft is a member of rather large diameter?"

"Precisely sixteen inches, like our own."

"Which necessarily would be the diameter of the hole through the sternpost?"

"Almost exactly."

"And the water is denied admittance how?"

"A plug is the usual contrivance to this end."

"An externally applied plug?"

"This is the best and easiest application."

"How might this plug be dislodged?"

Elias Quaner pursed his lips. "By any of several methods. A sharp blow, for instance."

"Would such a blow be difficult to administer?"

"By no means; a person so inclined need merely stand on the rudder and swing a mallet."

Zamp raised his glass. "To your health and the strength of Bonko's right arm! At an appropriate time we will discuss this matter again. In the meantime—not a word to anyone! Least of all your cousin aboard *Fironzelle's Golden Conceit*!"

"I understand completely."

At the door of the cabin sounded a rap-rap-rap. "Come!" called Zamp.

Chaunt the steward entered with an envelope of bright yellow paper. "This has just been handed aboard."

Opening the envelope, Zamp withdrew a sheet of yellow paper. He read:

> To the estimable Apollon Zamp:
>
> I speak for King Waldemar of Mornune. Your noble ship *Miraldra's Enchantment* being on hand, I invite your participation in a competition to be held tomorrow.
>
> The procedure is this: the master of each vessel shall present that program which he considers his best. An anonymous observer will adjudge each presentation and decide upon the most excellent. Programs will follow each upon the other, commencing at noon upon the *Two Varminies* to the north of the harbor, then proceeding south from boat to boat, to terminate upon the *Miraldra's Enchantment*.
>
> On the following morning the qualifying shipmaster will be notified, and an announcement will be posted on the notice board before The Jolly Glassblower.
>
> It is suggested that no entrance fee be levied upon the public for the performances of tomorrow, and that a lapse of fifteen minutes be allowed between programs, for the convenience of all.
>
> A noble prize at Mornune lies within the scope of tomorrow's victor! Each should strive to his best avail! Affixed below: the Seal of the House of Bohun.

The red seal attached to the yellow page depicted two griffins in a circle, each biting the other's tail.

Zamp handed the letter to Elias Quaner, who read the letter twice in the thorough fashion of the Quaners. "Our performance will follow that of Garth Ashgale, so it would appear."

"That would be my interpretation of the instructions. Our own drive shaft is securely in place?"

"It is indeed."

"Garth Ashgale is cursed with a fecund imagination. We must be vigilant. It might be wise to bring all the ship's company aboard for the rest of the day and night."

"A sensible precaution."

Osso Santelmus opened the competition with little more than a token performance. His clowns capered to raucous music; a magician caused objects to sprout wings and fly across the stage; Santelmus himself delivered a comic monologue and simulated a fight between two vulps and a grotock.

The next presentation, aboard the *Vissel Dominator*, was somewhat more ambitious: "The Legend of Malganaspe Forest" in sixteen tableaux. The *Psychopompos Revenant* staged a ballet: "The Twelve Virgins and Buffo the Lewd Ogre." The middle afternoon was enlivened by "Gazilda and his Unfortunate Double-jointed Idiots," on the *Fireglass Prism*. As Phaedra the sun settled into the Lant River, the troupe aboard the *Chantrion* staged a rather macabre burlesque: "The Oel's Dinner Party."

The merry population of Lanteen, unaccustomed to so generous a spate of free entertainment, next thronged aboard *Fironzelle's Golden Conceit*, where Garth

Ashgale's disciplined eight-piece orchestra played a lively mazurka.

Garth Ashgale came out on the stage and stood smiling in the focused glow of a dozen lamps. He wore a suit of rich dark blue velvet, a shirt of fine white lawn, the headdress of a Sarklentine mage. His manner was easy and suave; he held his hands up and apart to signal the orchestra to silence, and behind him the curtain drew aside a trifle to display a glimpse of the stage setting. "My dear friends of Lanteen! It is a great pleasure to bring my troupe before an audience so discriminating; I promise I will not insult either your intelligence or your sensibilities with trivial farce or mindless saltations or lewd contortions. No! This pleasant night I bring you the drama *Rorqual*: full, authentic and unexpurgated, complete with the awful death of the traitor Eban Zirl."

Thud. Standing in the bow of *Miraldra's Enchantment*, Zamp grimaced in apprehension. The sound had been somewhat louder than he expected. But Ashgale never paused in his remarks, and a moment later Bonko the boatswain crawled up a ladder from out of the dark water, to stand dripping on the deck immediately aft of the forepeak. He made a significant gesture to Zamp, then hauled on a line to bring a great steel mallet up on deck, which he carried forward into the boatswain's locker. Zamp returned his attention to the remarks of Garth Ashgale:

"—all realize the circumstances of this unique event. I sincerely hope that the noble observer from Mornune, whose identity is unknown to us, will derive from our performance that same sublime emotion which we, with all our hearts and faculties, have tried to put into it.

"So now: *Rorqual*!" The curtains parted to reveal one of Ashgale's most sumptuous stage settings.

"We find ourselves at Dalari Temple. The priestesses greet Prince Orchelstyne with music and chanting. From behind the columns of the temple appear the priestesses, weaving back and forth in a sinuous dance."

Bonko came to join Zamp at the bow. "What occurs?"

"The stern is starting to settle. Ashgale has still noticed nothing."

Ashgale intoned, "Prince Orchelstyne does not yet know that he has been chosen the ritual husband of the goddess Sofre. . . ."

Zamp said, "Now he wonders. . . . Now he suspects . . . . Now he is certain."

Fironzelle's Golden Conceit sagged stern-first into the river, and the throng which had so recently boarded the vessel surged ashore in tumult, while Ashgale ran back and forth across the stage shouting orders to his crew.

Zamp turned to Bonko. "Put a careful guard over our hawsers. Send Sibald aloft to inspect the stays and shrouds, then station a man at the rudder-post to warn off swimmers. I want a patrol of all passageways and the outboard gunwales. Keep everyone on alert!"

Bonko rushed off to comply with the orders. Aboard *Fironzelle's Golden Conceit*, Phinian Quarner the engineer had improvised a plug of wadded cloth to reduce the influx of water. The ship lay askew, its quarterdeck almost awash. Garth Ashgale ran in and out of his cabin, carrying forth scripts, records, clothes, mementoes, his strongbox. On shore the crowd watched for a few minutes, then, convinced that the vessel was not about to sink, began to file aboard *Miraldra's Enchantment*.

Zamp waited until the seats were occupied, then stepped out on his stage. "With great regret I have observed the unfortunate circumstances aboard the ship of my colleague Master Garth Ashgale. The mishap, of course, was not unexpected; we had discussed the deficiencies of his boat at Coble. In any event, all of us trust that the vessel will soon be repaired and back in service.

"So now, our own contribution to the entertainment of this remarkable day: first, our diverting fantasy *The Magic Box of Ki-chi-ri*."

Zamp stepped back; the curtains drew aside to reveal the workroom of Frulk the Magician. Coming on stage, Frulk went about his experiments to a crotchety music of squeaks and quavers. His goal was the transformation of flowers into beautiful maidens, but his most earnest efforts went for naught. First he produced swirling puffs of colored smoke, then a flight of white birds, then sprays of pyrotechnics. Frulk at last discerned his mistake and performed a comical dance of excitement. He arranged six cabinets in a row and within each placed a flower: an elanthis, a tea rose, a branch of barberry blossoms, a purple tangalang, a blue Xyth lily, a yellow daffodil.

With great care Frulk performed his magic; the musicians produced chords of expectancy. Frulk uttered the activating incantation and opened his cabinets; out stepped six beautiful maidens, and Frulk cavorted around the room in a high-stepping jig of pure joy, the maidens meanwhile performing their own ballet of wonder at the mobility of their bodies. Frulk, becoming amorous, sought to capture and clasp the maidens, but in wonder and innocence and alarm they eluded him.

All the while Frulk's shrewish wife Lufa had been peering down from a window high in the wall, displaying a variety of extravagant grimaces: shock, disgust, annoyance, vindictive resolve.

Frulk ran back and forth like a maniac; the girls dodged and danced away and at last all jumped back into their cabinets and slammed the doors. Frulk, snatching open the doors, discovered only the flowers he had placed there previously.

Frulk walked back and forth in cogitation, then made preparations to perform his magic again. Lufa entered the room and sent Frulk away on an errand. As soon as Frulk had departed, Lufa opened the cabinets, pulled forth the flowers, tore them apart, gnashed them with her teeth, ground them into the floor. Then from a basket she took noisome herbs: dog's-breath, slankweed, erflatus, rhume, zogma, carrion weed; these she placed in the cabinets and after a caper of wicked glee left the room.

Frulk entered and, assured of Lufa's absence, once again performed his sorcery. On tiptoe he approached the cabinets, poised himself to grasp the beauties as they emerged, reached forward and the doors to all the cabinets flew wide. Out leapt six grotesques. Frulk jumped back aghast, and as the orchestra played a maniacal two-step, the grotesques pursued Frulk around the room. Down came the curtain.

Bonko came to report to Zamp. "I have arranged guards. The hawsers were soaked with acid and cut with blades, ready to part and drift us out on the river."

Zamp snorted in annoyance. "That villain Ashgale has no conscience! The hawsers are mended?"

"As good as new."

"Continue the alert."

The curtain drew back on one of Zamp's famous tableaux. Twenty members of the troupe wearing black garments and black masks stood before a black backdrop holding colored targets on rods, to create geometrical intricacies. From the orchestra came a click-clacking of drums and a muffled tinkling of the vitrophon; with each accent of the rhythm, the targets shifted into a new pattern, an effect which after a few moments became hypnotic.

Bonko came running to find Zamp. "A fire in the forepeak! A phosphorus clock was buried under rags and hay!"

Zamp ran forward, to find billows of smoke pouring from the boatswain's locker. Deckhands formed a chain, passed buckets of water into the locker, and the fire was extinguished. Bonko told Zamp: "The timing was precise; someone intended to panic the audience!"

"Ashgale has the soul of a mad dog; nothing deters him! Maintain a most careful watch!"

The curtain descended on the tableau and jugglers came forth to provide a brief interlude, throwing disks out over the audience, which swooped in a circle and returned to the jugglers' hands.

Bonko again reported to Zamp. "Two men in voluminous robes sit yonder in the audience; I believe they carry concealed objects."

"Conduct them to the quarterdeck, search them and deal with them accordingly."

Bonko returned several minutes later. "Villains as I suspected! They carried cages of pests, vermin and fire-hornets, which they were about to release into the audience. We thrashed them and threw them into the river."

"Excellent," said Zamp. "Remain vigilant."

The curtain drew back to reveal the surface of an exotic planet. Two men descended in a simulated spaceboat; they marveled at the peculiar conditions and experienced a set of ludicrous mishaps. In the trees sat huge insects playing a weird music on bizarre instruments. The music stopped short as a group of near-nude, near-human creatures appeared, running on all fours. The creatures gamboled and frisked, and inspected the spacemen with affectionate curiosity. The insect musicians again played music; the running creatures performed an eccentric and rather lewd dance in which the spacemen joined. The dance became a bacchanalian frenzy.

The music stopped short. A portentous silence gripped the stage. The music resumed, now heavy, dark and ominous. A huge being appeared, half-animal, half-ogre. With a whip of a dozen thongs, it forced the running half-human creatures to acts of abasement. The spacemen watched aghast and presently killed the beast. The music erupted into horrid discords; the half-men leapt high in paroxysms of fury; they tore the spacemen to bits; then, to eerie, slow music, performed a hectic pavanne around the corpse of the beast-ogre, and the curtain fell.

From the outboard side of the ship came the sound of a thud, a series of hoarse yells and a splashing sound. Zamp went to investigate and Bonko explained the new disturbance. "Three men in a rowboat attempted to fasten an explosive object to our waterline. I dropped a large stone into their boat and they drifted away on the current."

"Ashgale has not been idle," said Zamp. "To no avail; our performance is close upon its end. But do not relax."

Zamp took up a position where he could inspect the audience. Among them was the emissary from Mornune: which? No indications existed; the incognito was effective.

The curtains parted on Zamp's traditionally rousing grand finale. The orchestra played at crescendo, the players marched, pranced and cakewalked; jugglers twirled flaming hoops; magicians discharged rockets.

Zamp stepped onto the stage and as the curtain fell,

performed a modest bow. "We hope that you have enjoyed our efforts to entertain you. Next time we pass our acquaintance will certainly be renewed. All aboard *Miraldra's Enchantment* wish you good evening."

Chapter 4

All night long Zamp was kept awake by the sounds of pumps and curses from *Fironzelle's Golden Conceit.* In the morning the vessel still sagged by the stern.

Zamp enjoyed an early breakfast in his cabin, then dressed with his usual care in dark gray breeches, a green jacket frogged with loops of crimson cord, a crimson and green cap. Zamp then disposed himself to await the announcement of the Mornune envoy.

Half an hour passed. Zamp strolled forward to observe the raising of *Fironzelle's Golden Conceit.* Water surged from hoses emerging through portholes. Ashgale was nowhere to be seen.

As Zamp sauntered back amidships, a young man in the ordinary costume of Lanteen mounted the gangplank. Zamp paused, and the young man approached. "You are Apollon Zamp, ship-master?"

"I claim that distinction."

"In such case, I carry a message which I must deliver into your hands." The young man brought forth a black plush case which he delivered to Zamp, and immediately departed the ship.

Zamp pursed his lips reflectively. He put the black plush case down upon a bench and looked at it from a safe distance.

Bonko came past and gazed wonderingly at Zamp. "What troubles you?"

"The case yonder. It might contain almost anything."

Bonko considered the case. "Well, we shall soon discover the truth. A moment while I fetch a pair of clamps."

Bonko went forward and returned with clamps and lengths of cord. He clamped the bottom of the case to the table, attached a second clamp to the lid and tied one end of the cord to this second clamp. The other end of the cord he took to the shrouds and carried aloft to the crow's nest.

Zamp went to stand behind the deckhouse.

"Ready?" called Bonko.

"Ready," replied Zamp.

Bonko pulled the cord, but the clamp fell off the case and the strategy failed.

Behind Zamp stood Garth Ashgale who had boarded the vessel unnoticed and now stood watching with raised eyebrows. "What in the world are you doing?"

Zamp cleared his throat and gave the bill of his cap a tug. "We are attempting to open the black case yonder."

Garth Ashgale frowned in puzzlement. "Surely there is an easier way?" He walked over to the case, picked it up and lifted the cover. "You exaggerated the difficulty of the act."

Zamp made no response. He took the case and lifted forth a rectangle of thin bright metal, inscribed with a message in clear black characters.

Be it known to all persons that Master Apollon Zamp, with his vessel *Miraldra's Enchantment* and the members of his crew, orchestra and entertainment troupe are invited to participate in the Grand Festival at Mornune commencing on the thirteenth day after the summer solstice of this year. Such being the case they are granted an absolute safe-conduct through the Mandaman Gates, across the Bottomless Lake, and at the town Mornune during the period of the festival, and for such time thereafter as may be required for easy and safe departure:

Ordained through and by the power of Waldemar, King of Soyvanesse.

"Ah yes," said Zamp. "I expected something of this sort." He handed the plaque to Ashgale, who read the message with a placid gaze.

"My congratulations," said Ashgale. He hefted the plaque and glanced absentmindedly toward the river; Zamp hastily recovered the silver rectangle. He heaved a deep breath, and somewhat grudgingly said, "The morning is fine; would you care to take a cup of tea?"

"I accept with pleasure," said Ashgale. The two strolled aft and climbed to the quarterdeck. Zamp arranged a pair of wicker chairs beside the massive chart table; the two men relaxed and stretched out their legs, while Chaunt served tea and biscuits.

"I was unable to attend your performance last night," said Ashgale. "We had an exasperating accident which caused considerable inconvenience. I understand that your show was up to usual standards: a clever concoction of froth, nudity and nonsense. Someday when I have exhausted the immediate urgencies of my intellect I might relax and play a season or two of farce and phantasmagoria, if for no other reason than variety."

"Excellent!" declared Zamp. "The field is difficult, because it demands a peculiar quality of exactness and subtlety which cannot be taught and cannot be learned.

Naturally I will help you as well as I can, but I warn you, I am a martinet.''

"We shall see, we shall see," said Ashgale negligently. "I have several months to form my plans, as I intend to return to Coble and give my ship a reconditioning." Ashgale sipped his tea. "What of yourself? The Mornune competition is still two months in the future."

Zamp gave the silver plaque a disdainful tap. "This is an amusing trophy, but I doubt if I will give it much heed. A pity I cannot transfer it to someone who truly wants such a trinket.''

Ashgale made a dubious grimace. "Mornune is far upstream. I doubt if many sensible folk would want to pursue a will-o'-the-wisp quite so far.''

Zamp signaled to Chaunt. "Bring up the *River Index*." To Ashgale he said, "I am curious; let us see exactly what the journey entails.''

Chaunt set the heavy brown volume on the table and Zamp flicked over the vellum pages. " 'Mornune: a rich town on Cynthiana Bay at the north end of Bottomless Lake, established by Merse Hawkmen from the Great Airy Plain north of Dragonsway, West-central Lune XXII. From Coble, Mornune may be best approached on the summer monsoon, which provides sufficient wind to counter the Vissel current. Departure conversely is most easily effected in the fall calms or during the winter monsoon. Eighteen to twenty-two days are required for the voyage in either direction. Along the Vissel will be found towns and villages of more or less importance, such as Prairie View, Idanthus, Port Venoble, Garken, Port Wheary, Orangetown, Cockaigne City, Oxyrhincus. Some of these places are fortified against the Tinsitala tribes; others are open and the inhabitants when beleaguered take to their boats or hide in the marshes.

" 'Important tributaries to the Vissel are the Murne at Wigtown, the Wergence near Gotpang, the Suanol at Fudurth, the Lant at Lanteen, the Trobois at Port Wheary.

" 'Tribes of hostile nomads occasionally appear along the shore and precautions must be effected; it is never wise to moor to the riverbank overnight.

" 'Mornune itself is notable for the elegance of its structures and the wealth of its ruling caste, who trace their lineage to Rorus Cazcar of the Magic Tabard.' " Zamp looked down the columns. "There's more here, but I imagine that you have studied your own *Index* at length."

Ashgale nodded graciously. "I have investigated the feasibility of the voyage, but without any real interest."

Zamp turned his gaze out across the Lant River and past, up the sparkling reaches of the Vissel where it came down from the north, far, far, to where it seemed that human vision must fail, and beyond, across the Big Planet perspectives, until the Vissel was no more than a wisp of silver thread.

"Aha," said Ashgale, "I see that you have determined to make the voyage."

"It is country I have never seen," mused Zamp. "There is a fortune awaiting me up yonder, if I choose to reach for it."

Ashgale looked out over the water with a rather bleak expression. "Well, I'll be faring south to Coble. You'll bide here at Lanteen?"

"And pay out a month of salaries? Not likely. The Lant River tempts me. Perhaps I'll fare out to Port Whant, or even Bilch and Funk's Grove."

"Port Whant is a morose place," mused Ashgale.

"You will discover there an audience only for tragic drama; they care not a fig for nonsense."

Zamp gave an austere nod. "So I am informed by the *Index*. I will no doubt present some suitable piece: perhaps my own *Evulsifer* or *The Legend of Lost Girl Mountain*."

Ashgale rubbed his chin. "Are you in the market for a criminal? I will sell one cheap: a surly fellow who barely troubles to learn his lines; in fact he was for last night's performance, but now I have no need for him."

"What are his particulars?"

"I bought him here at Lanteen: an adjudged rapacious murderer, and a villainous creature in truth. Pay me a hundred groats, if you like."

"A hundred groats? My dear Ashgale, I have no need for such an expensive adjunct; I can behead a dummy without charge."

"As you will. Reflect however on the man's expressive face, his hoarse voice, his baleful presence. A hundred groats is a cheap price to pay for such verisimilitude."

Zamp smilingly shook his head. "Master Ashgale, you have suffered reverses and I am inclined to sympathize with you; however, I cannot empty my strongbox so capriciously. I'll take him off your hands, but I wouldn't lay forth a single groat."

"Come now, Apollon Zamp!" said Ashgale. "Such rhetoric we both know to be absurd. Either make me a fair offer, or let us consider the subject closed."

Zamp shrugged. "I have never been one to haggle. I can offer ten groats, which should compensate you for your outlay."

"I maintain a rigid barrier between personal and business relationships," said Ashgale. "No matter what my regard for you, I cannot make so unfavorable a transaction."

Eventually the sum of twenty-two and two-thirds groats was agreed upon. Ashgale took his money and departed, and Zamp sent Bonko and four deckhands over to the *Fironzelle's Golden Conceit* with a cage, and presently the criminal was brought aboard the *Miraldra's Enchantment*.

Zamp looked into the cage and found the prisoner no more appealing now than before. "I deplore the crimes which have necessitated your punishment; nevertheless you will find me an indulgent host, especially if you undertake to deliver Evulsifer's final peroration at an appropriate moment."

"Save your breath," grumbled the prisoner. "You clearly intend to take my life; do your worst and be damned to you."

"This is fallacy," declared Zamp. "The death sentence was pronounced not by the management of this vessel, but by the town Lanteen. We can only transform the occasion from a sordid little affair in a cellar to exalted drama in which you perform an indispensable role. In your place I would cooperate with great zest."

"I will gladly change with you," said the prisoner. "Otherwise it is all one."

"Another matter," said Zamp. "The role personifies Evulsifer as a fair man of distinguished appearance—in fact I usually play the part myself, up to the moment of execution. You do not match this description, and I would wish to shave your beard, cut your hair, supply you with a wig and dress you in fine garments. Otherwise you must be executed in a black robe with a heavy cowl."

"I am not vain," said the man. "If you must execute

a popinjay, put your own head on the block and all requirements will be met."

Zamp said in disgust, "You are intractable. Solicit no favors from me."

The prisoner rattled the bars of his cage. "Look forward to your own death with foreboding! In the afterlife I plan to deal harshly with all my enemies!"

"I suspect that our future planes of existence will be quite distinct," said Zamp loftily, and walked away from the cage. He spent a moment reflecting upon the prisoner's threat. Could such things be? If so, what weird events must transpire in the afterlife! . . . Hmm. Here was material for a new drama.

At the bow he found Bonko. "Make ready for departure," said Zamp. "We sail up the Lanteen as soon as possible."

"I'll need an hour to comb the taverns," said Bonko.

"Departure time, then, will be noon."

Zamp returned to the quarterdeck, and consulted the *River Index* notes on Port Whant:

Originally settled by a tribe of white Nens, Port Whant is to this day notorious for the truculence of its citizens. The Whants nevertheless are not parsimonious and can be expected to provide enthusiastic audiences for high-quality productions. This very spontaneity of reaction however is a mixed blessing if the performance is shabby, mean, or inconsiderable, when the Whants may well make a vehement expression, or go so far as to demand refund, to which the wise ship-master will give instant accommodation.

The Whants are ruled by a warlord who leads them on their raids, and whom they hold in deepest reverence. The current warlord is Lop Loiqua, a man of considerable force.

Under no circumstance make facetious reference to the town, or to the warlord. The Whants in any case are a rather grim folk who dislike farce or travesty; tragic dramas such as *Xerxonistes* or *The Monster of Munt* are generally well received.

The Whants are most sensitive to color stimulation. Females should wear no yellow, as this is for the Whants a sexual excitant, and is considered a signal of invitation. Similarly men should wear no red, which might be interpreted as a challenge. Black is a color of debasement, worn by pariahs—

Chaunt the steward approached. "A person to see you, sir. She is waiting by the gangplank."

Zamp rose to his feet and peered down to the main deck, "Indeed, indeed. Show her to my cabin." Zamp set his jacket, and tugged his cap to the jauntiest angle possible. He waited a moment, then descended to the main deck and entered his cabin.

His visitor stood by the table, one hand resting on the umber surface. The two inspected each other for a moment, then Zamp doffed his cap and tossed it across the room in a gesture of gallant abandon. The young woman watched without expression, evincing neither interest nor approval. She wore a costume which set off her slender figure to excellent advantage: soft gray trousers, black ankle-boots, a flaring dark blue cape. Her glossy blonde hair was held in place by a loose-crowned black beret with a tassel hanging past her right ear. Zamp could find no clues in her garments or features as to her race, caste or place of origin. He said, "I believe that we have met before, at The Jolly Glassblower."

The young woman seemed a trifle puzzled and Zamp

asked himself, was it possible that she had not noticed him?

"This may well be. You are Apollon Zamp?"

"I claim that dubious distinction, indeed. What of yourself?"

"I wish to become a member of your troupe."

"Aha! Please be seated. Will you take a glass of wine?"

"Nothing, thank you." The young woman seated herself in the chair which Zamp brought forward. "You are naturally wondering as to my dramatic capabilities. They are not large, but on the other hand I demand no large salary."

"I see," said Zamp. "What in fact are these capabilities?"

"Well, I can no doubt act parts; I play a minor guitar with some facility, and I can give chess demonstrations."

"These are special talents, to be sure," said Zamp "Can you perform agile dances?"

"This is a skill in which I have not been trained," said the young woman rather haughtily.

"Hmm," said Zamp. "Do you know the tragic drama *Evulsifer*?"

"I fear not."

"The nude ghost of Princess Maude walks the parapets of Castle Doun during the second act. You might adequately command the role."

"The nudity is of course simulated?"

"Ghostliness is suggested by the use of a gossamer curtain. Nudity, however, is better portrayed by actuality than by simulation. Such has been our experience."

The young woman looked out the casements and across the water. Zamp studied her profile, which he found exquisite. "Ah well," she muttered, more to herself than Zamp, "what difference does it make?"

Zamp said: "You know my name, but you still have not enlightened me as to your own."

"You may address me as—" she hesitated and frowned. "It is a difficult matter to reconcile formality with convenience."

"Perhaps you could simply tell me your name."

"It is Damsel Tatwiga Berjadre Ilkin al Marilszippor cam Zatofoy dal Tossfleur cam Ysandra dal Attikonitsa al Blanche-Aster Wittendore."

"The pedigree is imposing," said Zamp. "I will call you Damsel Blanche-Aster. And where is your home-place?"

"My birthplace is Castle Zatofoy in the land of Wyst."

Zamp pursed his lips. "These places are not known to me."

"They are remote, as are the circumstances of my life, and I prefer not to discuss them."

"As you wish," said Zamp. "Now—if you are to join the troupe—you must adopt a possibly novel point of view. We function as a unit; we have no place aboard for acrimonious or abrasive personalities, diffidence, languor or excessive temperament. Prudence, discretion, restraint are indispensable qualities as we sail from town to town, inasmuch as each is different from the next and we can risk offending no one. For instance, at Port Whant you may wear no yellow, inasmuch as this will be regarded as receptivity to sexual proposals."

Damsel Blanche-Aster gave him a cold glance. "I am sure that such vulgar episodes are uncommon."

Zamp gave a casual laugh. "Not altogether. In fact, after a month or so, you will drop the words *common* and *uncommon* from your vocabulary."

Damsel Blanche-Aster sat looking off across the cabin and out the stern casements, and it seemed to Zamp that she was on the verge of rising to her feet and departing the ship. But she sighed and made some sort of internal adjustment, and Zamp breathed easier.

"As for your compensation," said Zamp, "I can offer you the wage of a part-player, which will be augmented as you demonstrate new skills. Aboard this ship I emphasize versatility, which I find to be stimulating for everyone."

Damsel Blanche-Aster gave an indifferent shrug. "As for my quarters, I prefer a cabin similar to this, with adjacent bathing facilities."

Zamp stared in wonder. "My dear young lady, no such similar cabin exists!" He essayed a facetious gallantry, which he immediately knew to be a mistake. "Unless of course you care to share this cabin with me." He added lamely, "Which might—ha—offend less fortunate members of the troupe."

Damsel Blanche-Aster ignored the suggestion as if it had not been made. Her voice frosted the air. "Essentially, I require only privacy; if necessary, I am willing to put up with inconvenience."

Zamp pulled at his blonde goatee. "In view of your obvious gentility, you may take your meals here with me in this cabin. On the deck below is a spacious lazarette, conveniently adjacent to my private bath, which can be used as a cabin. It is not particularly airy nor bright, but nowhere else aboard ship can I provide the privacy you request."

"It must suffice. I will order my effects aboard at once."

"We depart at noon; please make haste."

Zamp escorted Damsel Blanche-Aster out on deck and with a warm weakness of the joints watched her leave the ship. He shook his head in wonder. A marvel, a nonesuch, a rarity! He craned his neck to look after her erect, supple form as she walked along the esplanade. A creature beautiful as the dawn, luminous with intelligence. Even her hauteur was fascinating! But no denying a profoundly strange quality to the situation, which only a simpleton could ignore! Why would such a remarkable person opt for the life of a showboat player? A mystery which he would endeavor to resolve, along with all her other mysteries and reticences. Zamp considered the days to come with a thrill of anticipation, as if he had returned to adolescence and were experiencing the pangs of infatuation.

Summoning Chaunt, Zamp gave instructions as to the lazarette, then returned to the quarterdeck and pretended to study the *River Index*.

. . . Bilch, like other communities up and down the Vale of Lant, must constantly stay on the alert against the rapacity of the Whants, and in consequence has evolved a curious psychology compounded of nervousness and fear, repressed hostility, and the ordinary human need for self-assertion and pride. The folk of Bilch therefore seem almost disoriented and victims of confused impulses. The official who one moment gives an obsequious greeting may on the next turn to snarling and gnashing his teeth like a cur. On the other hand, the gang of furtive youths who in the shelter of darkness pelt the visitor with rocks might well perform prodigies of selfless valor to save him from drowning. . . .

Members of the troupe straggled up the gangplank, removing the pegs opposite their names on the roster board as they stepped on deck. A pair of porters brought Damsel Blanche-Aster's belongings aboard: three varnished rattan cases with iron clips and hinges—rich

cases indeed! Zamp strolled forward to the bow, not
wishing to be in evidence when Damsel Blanche-Aster
herself came aboard. For a day or two he would maintain a courteous distance, almost an aloofness. Such an
attitude would intrigue her imagination and stimulate
her female predacity. She would wonder where and
how she was lacking and exert herself to be captivat-
ing. . . . Garth Ashgale, on the quarterdeck of his
Fironzelle's Golden Conceit, called across the water:
"So then: you are faring forth?"

"I am indeed. And you?"

"I must make repairs, worse luck, or I'd be up the
Lant myself. How far up do you venture?"

"I have not yet decided."

"Good luck then and large audiences. What will you
play at Port Whant?"

"*Evulsifer*, though we are rusty at the roles."

"An excellent choice! The Whants are a dismal lot.
Give them gore and they'll never notice the deficien-
cies." Garth Ashgale—smiling rather broadly, thought
Zamp—waved his hand and turned away.

Damsel Blanche-Aster came aboard. She halted a
moment, looked right and left along the decks, up and
down the masts, then sauntered aft to the quarterdeck,
to stand leaning on the taffrail looking north up the
brimming Vissel.

Bullocks were harnessed to the capstan; Zamp gave
the order to cast off lines: *Miraldra's Enchantment*
eased out upon the Lant. Zamp ordered all sails set; on
a broad reach the ship drove up-river. Damsel Blanche-
Aster came up behind Zamp. "Master Zamp, if you
please!"

Zamp turned to find Damsel Blanche-Aster's face
puzzled and uncertain. She asked: "Where are we going?
The Vissel flows yonder!"

"Exactly. This is the Lant. We will present entertainments at certain of the upstream towns."

"But are you not sailing north to play at the Grand Festival?"

"I have not definitely decided. All in all, I think not. The way is long and the outcome uncertain."

"But you gained King Waldemar's invitation!"

"The festival is still two months distant; there is time to spare if I change my mind."

Damsel Blanche-Aster looked back toward Lanteen, then went thoughtfully to a wicker chair and seated herself.

Zamp pulled up a chair and settled beside her. "This afternoon we begin rehearsals for *Evulsifer*. I play a part in this drama; in fact I myself will be Evulsifer."

"And I must walk nude today across the battlements?"

"Only if such a condition pleases you."

Damsel Blanche-Aster gave a curt nod. "I have resigned myself to indignities, which I trust you will try to minimize."

"You speak with such dire foreboding! I intend that you shall enjoy yourself. Do you know, I have yet to see you laugh?"

Damsel Blanche-Aster turned him a level glance. "Why should you concern yourself? We are utter strangers."

"Not quite!" declared Zamp. "I reject this theory!" He reflected that his policy of reserve and aloofness had not proved feasible. "My position is a lonely one. Now, suddenly, you are here: a person of beauty and intelligence. Is it a miracle that I should wonder at your disconsolate expression? Or that I should point out how the sun scintillates along the waves; how perfectly the white sails swell and sweep against the blue sky; how pleasant it is to sit here and raise a finger to Chaunt for tea or iced punch or whatever is wanted?''

Damsel Blanche-Aster deigned a faint smile. "Chaunt unfortunately is not omnipotent.''

"You require something beyond his capacity? What might it be? . . . No, don't tell me. Perhaps I don't really want to probe your mysteries." Zamp waited, watching her covertly sidewise, but she made no response, merely sat gazing pensively across the water.

For a period the two sat in silence. Zamp spoke at last. "A word about your role. It is both easy and demanding. You have no lines to speak, but you must project a spectral intimation; you must awe the audience with a chill of the unknown.''

"I have seen ghosts walk at Castle Zatofoy. There is no difficulty to the matter.''

"Permit me to ask why, rather than residing at this noble castle, you are now here on the Lant River?''

"The simplest of reasons. The castle was conquered. My family was killed. I am lucky to have escaped with my life. There is now no more Castle Zatofoy; it was burned, then broken apart stone from stone.''

Zamp shook his head sympathetically. "There are worse fates than life aboard *Miraldra's Enchantment*.''

"Doubtless.''

Chaunt the steward appeared. "Where shall I lay out lunch, sir?''

"In the cabin. The honorable Damsel Blanche-Aster will be taking her meals with me.''

At lunch Damsel Blanche-Aster was as uncommunicative as before; Zamp noted, however, that she ate with a good appetite.

During the afternoon the troupe rehearsed *Evulsifer* and Zamp was not displeased with the effort. Damsel

Blanche-Aster walked the battlements in a most satis-factory style; Bonko, in the role of executioner, beheaded a dummy with satisfying precision.

During the evening meal Damsel Blanche-Aster seemed somewhat more relaxed. Zamp, however, took pains not to press too hard at intimacy. When the table had been cleared, Zamp poured two goblets of amaranthine liquor and brought a small guitar from his cabinet. "I would like to hear you play, if it pleases you to do so."

Damsel Blanche-Aster unenthusiastically took the gui-tar, fingered the strings and placed it on the table. "It is tuned incorrectly."

"Tell me how you prefer the tuning."

Damsel Blanche-Aster herself tuned the guitar, then played a slow, simple melody to a twanging of rhyth-mic chords. "The song has words, which I have forgot-ten." She again placed the guitar on the table and rose to her feet. "I am not in the mood to play; please excuse me." She left the cabin.

Zamp followed her out on deck. The sun had set behind the low banks of the Lant; twilight sky reflected on the water. Zamp called Bonko and gave orders for the evening: "The wind seems fresh and fair; we will sail until night grows dark, then anchor in the stream. Put out robber nets and post a four-man lookout. This is nomad country, and vigilance is necessary."

Zamp took the guitar to the quarterdeck and sat for a half-hour playing idle chords, but Damsel Blanche-Aster, after standing at the bow, returned aft and went below to her cabin.

Chapter 5

On the afternoon of the second day out of Lanteen Port Whant appeared on the north bank: a cramped cluster of two- and three-storied houses constructed of timber and plastered stone, with roofs meeting and joining and slanting at every angle. Zamp had arrayed *Miraldra's Enchantment* in its most festive guise. Screens of withe and wood towered above the midship gunwales to suggest an imposing castle; aloft fluttered flags and bunting of white and green, the colors least offensive to the Whants.

With maximum display, *Miraldra's Enchantment* approached the Port Whant dock, flags fluttering, tumblers cartwheeling to the music of belphorns, drums and screedles. Back and forth across the triatic stay marched acrobats carrying advertising placards and the emblem of Port Whant. The girls of the troupe lined the parapets of the simulated castle, wearing gowns of pale blue, to indicate a state of demure chastity.

A dozen or so folk from the town sauntered out upon the docks. They wore shapeless cloaks of dark brown furze and stood in small silent groups; Zamp signaled his troupe to even greater efforts.

The boat glided up to the dock; hawsers were dropped over bollards; the vessel was warped close to the dock and made secure. Meanwhile the troupe exerted itself to the utmost. The tumblers leaped, caracoled, turned back-flips; the acrobats pretended to fall from the stay, catching themselves by one last grasp; the girls, now in transparent hip-length smocks of pale blue gauze, to combine the maximum titillation with the minimum provocation, leapt back and forth across the upper windows of the simulated castle.

More folk from the town came out on the dock, hunched in a dour and almost sullen silence. Zamp was not discouraged; each community along the river had its distinctive style, and Port Whant was notoriously wary with strangers.

The gangplank was lowered to the dock; Zamp stepped out upon the landing. He looked back over his shoulder and gave a merry flourish of arm and hand; the frenzied demonstration instantly halted and the members of the troupe gratefully descended to the main deck.

Zamp paused a moment, the better to focus the attention of his audience. He wore one of his most elaborate costumes: a wide-brimmed brown hat with a great orange plume; a doublet striped orange and black belted over loose brown breeches, foppish knee-high boots precisely creased and pleated. The faces looking up from the dock expressed neither hostility nor friendliness nor even much interest; Zamp felt only a condition of introverted gloom. Hardly a handsome folk, he thought; both men and women showed pale, broad faces, lank black hair, heavy black eyebrows, burly physiques. Still, for all the apparent uniformity of garb and appearance, the sense of personality and self-autonomy was strong: perhaps as a result of the brooding melancholy which Zamp now determined to dispel. He held up his hands. "Friends of Port Whant! I am Apollon Zamp; this is my marvelous showboat *Miraldra's Enchant-*

ment. We have voyaged up the Lant to bring you one of our unparalleled entertainments.

"Tonight we plan a program which for sheer grandeur may never be surpassed in the long and glorious history of Port Whant!

"Citizens! Tonight we present not one, not two, but a three-part program, each part of supreme elegance. First: the Birdmen, or so they call themselves, for they literally seem to fly through the air. Gravity is no more to them than dirt to a chicken; they leap, they plunge, they hurtle and somersault with grace and aplomb. Secondly, we plan to perform a mischievous little trifle, still totally decorous and nonprovocative, entitled *The Love-ways of Far Climes and Far Times*. I suggest ladies and gentlemen, that you will be amazed by these absolutely authentic customs—but, naturally, it is all in good fun; our girls wear pale green and pale blue and are merely playing saucy jokes. If anyone considers such a program offensive or suggestive, please communicate with me, and we will substitute an equally amusing alternate piece. Third, and the high point of the evening: that famous drama of hate and passion and woe *Evulsifer!* You will experience poignant realism; you will witness the betrayal of a king, a palace orgy, the death of a traitor in its grisly actuality: a program to edify and instruct the discriminating folk of Port Whant!

"For this grandiose entertainment are we demanding a vast and unreasonable sum? By no means! A single groat per person allows participation in this moving experience. So then! In one hour let us have the entire population of Port Whant here at the dock! Time for all to go home, to spread the news to friend and neighbor, to bring all the family aboard our wonderful showboat!"

Zamp raised his hand; the orchestra played a fanfare. "In one hour, then, this gangplank will conduct you into a world of colored lights and wonderful happenings! Thank you, my friends, for your attention!'' Zamp bowed and swept his plumed hat to the deck. The Whants muttered to each other, and presently departed the dock.

"An odd group!" Zamp told Bonko. "They seem bloodless and apathetic, as if just risen from their deathbeds.''

"What says the *River Index?*'' asked Bonko.

"The Whants are described as a fiery folk, quick to resent insult. These Whants act as if they had been converted to a religion of abnegation and piety.''

"Here comes an old man; why not put the question to him?''

Zamp inspected the man approaching along the dock. "In all candor, I am reluctant to put any questions to anyone for fear of provoking annoyance. Still, this man seems mild enough.''

Zamp descended to the dock and waited until the old man hobbled past. "Good afternoon, Grandfather; what is the news at Port Whant?''

"The news is as always,'' stated the old man. "Murder, capture, defeat, and mischief. Why are you so concerned with our tragedy?''

"Only so that my company may help assuage your grief,'' was Zamp's glib reply. Evidently even the oldsters could not be taken lightly. "Our drama *Evulsifer* may well purge your souls of useless emotion.''

"Easier said than done. Lop Loiqua is gone, the victim of treachery, and part of our souls are gone with him. Where will we find another to take his place; he who was known as the Scourge of the Vale? The arrival of your boat may well be an omen.''

"Such it is!'' declared Zamp heartily. "An omen of entertainment, but no more!''

"Surely you would not think to dictate how we must read omens?"

"By no means! I only ventured to suggest—"

"Your suggestions are irrelevant; you know nothing of us and our habits."

"I agree with all you say; my only intent is to ensure your good opinion of myself."

The old man turned on his heel and limped away, only to pause after a few steps and look back over his shoulder. "I will say only this, that your insistent arguments would certainly provoke a man less obsessed with grief than myself!" He went his way. Zamp thoughtfully climbed the gangplank. He summoned his troupe and made an announcement:

"A word regarding our performance tonight and our general conduct. The folk of Port Whant are neither easy nor expansive. Attempt no familiarities; answer all questions 'yes' or 'no' with a suitable honorific; offer no opinions of your own! The females must wear no hint of yellow, the men must strip from their garments every trace of red. Black is a color of shame and debasement; offer nothing black to a Whant! Do not look at the audience lest they suspect a glare; maintain mild pleasant expressions, but do not affect a smile which might be considered derision. Immediately after the performance we will depart; I would do so now did I not fear their revenge. All now into costumes; play your parts with skill!"

Zamp went aft to his cabin and refreshed himself with a glass of wine. On the quarterdeck stood Damsel Blanche-Aster. Zamp finished his wine and joined her. "Did you hear my remarks? Even as a naked ghost you must display tact."

Damsel Blanche-Aster seemed bitterly amused. "It is

enough that I must display myself before these louts. Must I also appeal to their better natures?"

"If possible, yes! Walk slowly, with an abstracted air; the part need not be overplayed. It is time to get into your costume."

"In due course. The evening is not warm."

Zamp went to confer once more with Bonko. "It goes without saying that our emergency system is at the ready."

"Yes, sir. The pumps are manned; bullocks are at the capstan; crews are stationed at the under-jacks."

"Very good; be vigilant."

Half an hour passed. Despite their preoccupations, Whants began to assemble on the dock, and when Zamp opened the wicket, they paid the not inconsiderable price of admission without complaint and in an orderly fashion took their seats on the midship deck.

Zamp made the briefest of welcoming speeches and the evening's program began. Zamp was pleased with his tumblers and acrobats; never had they performed with such precision. The audience, though somewhat sullen, responded with mutters of amazement to some particularly daring feat. All in all, Zamp was well pleased.

The second section of the performance began as smoothly. In deference to the Whants, Zamp had truncated certain of the scenes and altered others, so that essentially the pastiche was little more than a series of courtships, performed in quaint costumes and with whatever picturesque elaborations Zamp had been able to contrive. The audience seemed mildly amused, but showed fervor only at those mildly erotic passages which Zamp had left intact. Still, no one complained or seemed uncomfortable and again Zamp felt that his audience was pleased with the show.

Zamp delivered the prologue to *Evulsifer* with a long blue cape hiding his costume. The orchestra played an obbligato of themes from the musical score, and Zamp, now somewhat less apprehensive, prepared for the first act almost with anticipation. Swince had outdone himself with his settings. The great salon at Asmelond Palace was splendid in scarlet and purple and green; the costumes of King Sandoval and his courtiers were almost too splendid.

The court intrigues at first seemed inconsequential; then subtly they began to propel the plot until King Sandoval and Prince Evulsifer were caught in tides of emotion they could not control.

Zamp staged the palace orgy with rather more latitude than he had originally planned, but the audience showed only approval, and when the rebel Trantino rose up behind the throne to stab King Sandoval, they hissed in horror.

The second act occurred on the Plain of Goshen before Gade Castle, where Evulsifer, accused of complicity in the death of his father, had taken refuge.

In front of the castle the action swirled. Evulsifer fought three duels with successively more ferocious opponents, then came forth by moonlight* for a tryst with his beloved Lelanie. He sang a wistful song to slow chords from his guitar; she swore devotion as changeless as the love which the fabled Princess Azoë had borne for her lover Wylas. And now Lelanie drew back in horror and pointed up to the battlements. "There walks the ghost of Agoë! It is a portent!"

Zamp also drew back to inspect the battlements and to gauge the quality of Damsel Blanche-Aster's perfor-

---

*Big Planet has no moon; however the concept of moonlight, with all its romantic associations, is engraved deep within the Big Planet psyche.

mance. A curtain of gauze surreptitiously dropped through the dimness blurred the image for the audience; Zamp however was afforded a better view, if from an inconvenient perspective; in any event, he had no fault to find with the quality of this ghost.

The ghost disappeared; Zamp somewhat mechanically spoke his lines and the act concluded with his capture through the perfidy of Lelanie.

Act Three opened with Evulsifer in chains, facing his accusers; he railed and challenged to no effect; he was sentenced to death and chained to a post, and left in solitude. Evulsifer delivered his tragic soliloquy and now Lelanie appeared on the set and the two performed that ambiguous scene which can be played in dozens of ways. Had she come to taunt him and mortify his distress? Was her heart balanced between love and guilt, cruelty and repentance? Did some evil madness compel her to evil? In the end Lelanie approached Evulsifer and tenderly kissed his forehead, then drew back and spat in his face; laughing almost hysterically she fled the scene.

Evulsifer must die at sunrise. Already the sky was flushed with dawn. He spoke his final dismal soliloquy and looked up to the platform where Bonko, costumed and masked as an executioner, prepared his axe and block.

Rays from the sun slanted over the horizon; Evulsifer was unchained from the post. A black cloak was thrown around him and a black hood pulled down over his head, and he was led out through the back of the stage, where the prisoner, similarly cloaked and hooded, had been brought from his cage.

"Must you be so brusque?" he demanded. "Hold back! I have scratched my arm on this splinter; bring me a bandage!"

"A trifle, a trifle," said Bonko. "This way, if you will."

The prisoner only kicked and struck out with his elbows; a gag was thrust between his teeth and he was dragged up to the platform where he struggled and groaned in a satisfactorily dramatic manner; four men fought to thrust him down with his neck on the block, dislodging his hood.

The executioner raised his axe; the first rays of the sun shone across the stage. "Strike!" cried the traitor Toraphin. The executioner struck; the head parted from the body, fell free of the hood, bounced off the platform, rolled across the stage to stare out at the audience. Very untidy, thought Zamp; the illusion had been somewhat damaged. Nonetheless, the audience had been profoundly affected; indeed they seemed paralyzed; all sat with bulging eyes fixed on the head. Peculiar, thought Zamp.

Someone spoke aghast in a voice half-moan, half-whisper: "Lop Loiqua."

Someone else hissed between clenched teeth: "Killed while in black."

Into Zamp's mind burst a single name: Garth Ashgale.

No time now for dismay. Zamp threw down cloak and hood and called to Bonko: "Stand by to cut the hawsers! Start up the beasts! Ready to make sail! I'll talk to the audience." Bonko lumbered off to deal with three tasks at once; Zamp mounted to the stage.

"Ladies and gentlemen—gallant Whants all—this concludes our entertainment for the evening. Please file from the ship in an orderly fashion. Tomorrow we present an amusing and inspiring program of agilities and magics—," Zamp ducked. Past his ear hurtled an ax. The audience had gained their feet. Each rage-distended face was fixed upon him; men and women scrambled over each other, clumsy and disoriented, intent only on laying hands on Apollon Zamp.

Zamp sprang aft and pulled the alarm gong; the troupe, drilled a hundred times to such a contingency, reacted with precision. Deckhands cut the hawsers; the vessel drifted away from the dock. Latches on the gunwales were pulled; the rails fell back and over, to hang down beside the hull. Below decks acrobats, magicians and stewards worked great screw jacks to raise the deck in half-sections so that each section sloped out toward the water. The bullocks turned the capstan to power the pumps; blasts of water tumbled the Whants down the sloping decks into the dark river.

A few, nevertheless, gained the foredeck. Some grappled the deckhands at the nozzles and flung them over the side. Others ran forward, toppled the great bow-lamp and threw torches up at the sails. Others brought oil from the forepeak and poured it across the decks; flame blasted high into the night. Zamp bawled down into the hold: "Reverse the jack; lower the deck!" but the troupe, appalled by the flames, clambered out of the hold and joined Zamp on the quarterdeck.

The entire bow of the boat seethed with flames. Whants ran crazily back and forth, yelling and hooting. The open hold deterred them from attacking the quarterdeck and they were finally forced by the flames to jump overboard.

"Down river!" roared Zamp. "We'll ride the current as far as we can. Man the pumps! To the fire hoses!"

But no one cared to venture down into the hold, under the burning rigging.

"Downstream with all speed!" cried Zamp, waving Evulsifer's sword defiantly toward Port Whant. "We'll drive our good ship as far as she'll carry us, then we'll beach her and let any who molest us beware!"

Bonko, still wearing his executioner's costume, politely disputed the order. "Better that we take to the boats, sir! If we beach, the boats may be burnt with the ship and tomorrow the Whants will ride us down."

Zamp threw aside the useless weapon and bleakly gazed forward at the roaring flames. "This is how it must be. Stand by to lower boats; we'll ride the old craft till she falters then let her go her own way."

Bonko ran off, shouting orders and instructions; Zamp retired to his cabin. He tore off his costume and donned a suit of gray twill, a fisherman's cap and sturdy boots; he belted on his best steel-pointed rapier, shoved a pair of snapples into his waistband together with a magazine of darts and charges. He stood in the center of his cabin and looked all around him, half-blinded by grief and fury. All within the range of his vision was precious: scripts, masks, mementos, testimonials, trophies, his carved furniture and fine blue carpet; his strongbox. . . . He rummaged in his chest and found a lank leather pouch into which he poured all his iron: five pounds or more. What else? He could take nothing else; all must burn. Someday he would own another vessel, the grandest on the river; he'd want no sad recollections, nothing to remind him of the old *Miraldra's Enchantment* save possibly the head of Garth Ashgale mounted on a plaque like a hunting trophy. . . . He had almost forgotten his jewels! He crossed to his dressing table and transferred the contents of his jewelbox to his pocket: a topaz and galena clasp, a wristlet of gold set with amethysts and iron studs, a silver chain with a great peridot cabochon; an emerald earclip; the silver tablet inviting his presence at the Mornune Festival; a contrivance of iron bars which he usually wore dangling and jingling from the side of his soft black velvet cap: all into his pocket; and now there was time for nothing more. Zamp slung the leather pouch over his shoulder and returned to the quarterdeck.

Bonko had worked with efficiency; at each of the four boats stood a complement of troupe and crew, awaiting orders to launch the lifeboats. Somewhat to the side, aloof and disinterested, Damsel Blanche-Aster waited with a bundle of her own belongings. Forward, the flames raged and crackled, illuminating the surface of the Lant: a dramatic and awful spectacle.

Bonko approached. "We must take to the boats. The planks are springing away from the stem and we're taking water forward; we might go down in a dive."

"Very good, lower the boats. Make sure the animals are released; give them a chance to swim for their lives."

The boats were lowered: three pinnaces and the somewhat more comfortable captain's gig, to which Zamp assigned Damsel Blanche-Aster. She climbed down the ladder and Zamp passed her bundle down to Chaunt the steward, then handed down his own heavy leather pouch. "Chaunt, make sure of this pouch; secure it in the forward cuddy!"

"Yes, sir!"

Zamp was last to leave the ship, already wallowing to the action of the water taken aboard. He climbed down into the gig. "Cast off!"

Oars were shipped; the boats pulled away from the flaming hulk. Zamp gazed steadfastly downstream, unwilling to watch the passing of his proud vessel. Flickering orange light played over his shoulder, brightening the fascinated faces of those who chose to look back.

In sudden puzzlement Zamp looked from person to person: where was Chaunt? Not in the gig. Odd. There he was in the pinnace a few feet to port. Zamp called across: "Chaunt! Where is my pouch?"

"Safe aboard the gig, sir, stowed in the forward cuddy."

"Very well."

The boats rounded a bend; Zamp took a last glance over his shoulder. Whants, rather than pursuing in their own boats, had paused to plunder the sinking ship; Zamp could see their dark shapes jumping with simian agility back and forth in front of the flames.

The riverbank obscured his vision; *Miraldra's Enchantment* was no more than a flickering glare in the sky. Presently even this was gone.

Chapter 6

All night the boats drifted down-river, rowing from time to time, the better to outdistance any Whants who might be pursuing.

At dawn the boats put ashore on a sandy river bar, to facilitate the stepping of masts and yards. Bonko built a fire, at which the troupe toasted sand-crawlers while the crew rigged the four boats.

Zamp noticed Damsel Blanche-Aster sitting with her bundle beside her and bethought himself of his pouch in the forward cuddy. It demonstrated a most gratifying weight, and Zamp stowed it again, more securely.

Returning to the beach he noticed that a number of crew members had gathered around Bonko, each seeming to make some insistent point. A few yards along the beach, the performers and musicians of the troupe were engaged in a similarly intense discussion.

A moment later Bonko and Viliweg the Master of Miracles presented themselves before Zamp. Viliweg spoke. "A rather interesting point has been raised by certain artists of the troupe—"

"And also by the members of the crew," said Bonko, who still wore the executioner's costume.

"—to the effect," continued Viliweg, "that once we reach Lanteen, a degree of confusion and flux will ensue and conceivably, through some error, salaries and wages might not be paid.''

Bonko said, ''The crew also feels that now is as good a time as any to settle up accounts, so that when we arrive at Lanteen no one need be inconvenienced.''

Viliweg endorsed the remark. ''The effort of searching out so many individuals at Lanteen in order to render to each his wage would be a most unfair vexation for a man already burdened with concern.''

Zamp looked from one to the other in amazement. ''I can hardly believe my ears! Return to your people and announce that my first and most urgent task is the acquisition of a new boat, so that all may once more be secure in their careers. With this concept in mind, I propose to retain the ship's monies in trust for all of us.''

Viliweg cleared his throat. ''Several members of the troupe predicted that you would entertain such ambitions. I agree that they are altruistic; unfortunately they are also visionary, and in short each member of the troupe requires his or her iron now.''

''The crew,'' said Bonko, ''holds to a similar point of view.''

Zamp shook his head in vexation. ''This attitude is so crass! Have we lost all sense of common purpose? Only by working together and perhaps sacrificing together can we achieve our goals!''

Viliweg spoke in a kindly voice. ''This program wins my support, but it must be implemented in the following manner. Each person will now receive his total remuneration, plus a hardship bonus and compensation for the loss of his personal effects. Then, when opportunity presents itself, we will again join our funds and our unique talents, to the advantage of all. No other procedure is possible.''

Zamp made an angry gesture. "I never thought to encounter such sordid and self-defeating obstinacy! The taverns at Lanteen will be the only ones to profit. Still, if you persist in your folly, I am forced to oblige you. I must mention in passing that when I select personnel for my new boat I will not be moved by sentiment or loyalty based on previous association."

"These events are still but dream-wisps in the mind of the Great Web-weaver," declared Viliweg. "Pay out the iron."

"Very well," said Zamp in a sullen voice. "Form a line in single file. Viliweg, you will be so good as to prepare a joint acknowledgement of payment, which each individual will sign as he or she receives his wages."

"Gladly," said the magician. "I believe that among my effects I carry paper and a stylus."

"One final remark," said Zamp. "Mention was made of 'bonuses' and 'compensation for losses.' At this time I can undertake no such extravagance. Employment terminated last evening, upon the stroke of Bonko's axe; payment shall be made only to this moment."

Zamp's declaration was not popular, and awoke considerable protest, which he ignored. Boarding the gig, he put ashore a bench to use for a counting table, then from the cuddy took his leather pouch, and jumped back to the beach.

"Very well," he called. "One at a time, approach, receive your iron, sign the document, and move aside. Do not attempt to rejoin the line, if you please. Complaints or disputes must be deferred until we reach Lanteen. Who is first: you, Viliweg?"

"Yes; since I will be supervising the signatures, it is most efficient that I be paid first. You owe me for precisely two months, four days, eleven hours and sixteen minutes.''

"What!" cried Zamp. "What nonsense is this! Have you forgotten the advance of thirty-three groats made to you at Lanteen?''

"Thirteen groats," roared Viliweg in return. "I asked for fifty; you claimed that you could only spare thirteen from the petty cash.''

"Not so! You also owe for a chit on ship's stores for approximately eleven groats, which I must deduct. Also—''

"A moment, a moment!" cried Viliweg. "Indeed I drew upon ship's stores for a pot of hair pomade, a blanket for my bed and a carton of preserved figs. All these have been destroyed in the fire; I have had neither use nor enjoyment of these items!''

Zamp shook his head decisively. "The debt exists. Also, you have miscalculated the span of time subject to remuneration by three weeks and four days. I find that I owe you, in round figures, the sum of sixty-seven groats. Please sign the document.''

Viliweg raised his clenched hands into the air. Accustomed to excesses of artistic temperament, Zamp paid no heed. Opening his pouch in a businesslike manner, he poured forth the contents upon the bench, the contents consisting of six heavy stones.

Zamp gazed down in consternation, then rose slowly to his feet. He looked down the line of folk waiting for their pay. Near the end stood Chaunt the steward.

Zamp called out, "Chaunt, be so good as to step this way.''

Chaunt came forward. "Yes, sir, what is the trouble?''

"When I handed this pouch down to you it contained five pounds of iron. Now I find only stones. How do you explain this situation?''

Chaunt's face expressed bewilderment. "I have no explanation whatever! I handed the bag to the juggler Barnwick and asked him to stow it in the cuddy—"

"I never handled the pouch!" declared Barnwick sharply. "You are mistaken!"

"Well, it was either you or someone similar," said Chaunt. "In the darkness and confusion I might well be mistaken."

"Chaunt, bring forward the case you are carrying. I wish to inspect the contents."

Chaunt made a mulish refusal. "I decline on two counts: first, I am a man of honor and I do not care to have my veracity questioned. Secondly, the case contains my life's savings, which an unreasonable man might identify as the missing iron."

Zamp reflected a moment. The concept of the wastrel Chaunt possessing savings of any kind was absurd. On the other hand, if he now undertook to regain his iron, he must instantly pay it out to see the coin lost once and for all. The time and place to deal with Chaunt was Lanteen. He spoke to the erstwhile troupe and crew. "My funds have been preempted. I am temporarily unable to satisfy your demands. I suggest that, rather than deploring our misfortunes, we pool our assets, both of talent and funds, in order to renew our destinies. Meanwhile, let us now proceed to Lanteen before the Whants find us here on the beach."

"Not so fast," said Chaunt. "I have my paltry savings, true, but I also want my pay. What, may I ask, bulges your pockets out to such an extent?"

"A few personal effects," said Zamp.

"Jewels and iron from your case?"

"They must be shared!" declared Viliweg. "Give them into the custody of a faithful trustee, such as

Bonko or myself, and at Lanteen we will distribute the proceeds."

"By no means," said Zamp and stood back, fingers hooked in his waistband, convenient to his snapples. "My trinkets are my own. To the boats!"

Without enthusiasm the troupe resumed their places, all except Chaunt. Zamp called, "Are you coming?"

"I think not," said Chaunt. "The motion of the boat makes me uneasy. I will walk the riverbank to Lanteen; it is only a few miles."

"I will stay and keep Chaunt company," said Bonko, and jumped ashore.

"Whatever you like," said Zamp, and pushed off from the beach.

Chaunt called out in sudden concern, "On second thought, I think I will ride the boat."

Someone cried, "Here come the Whants! They ride along the bank!"

"Out oars!" yelled Zamp. "Row for your lives! Hoist the sails!"

Along the banks pounded a troop of Whants bent low over their black horses, cloaks flapping behind them. Bonko and Chaunt fled along the bank, but were overtaken and cut down. The Whants fitted arrows to their short bows but the boats had gained the center of the river past effective range.

For an hour the Whants rode along the bank beside the boats, then saw no profit in the exercise and returned the way they had come.

Thrust along both by the current and a fair wind the boats moved at speed, and just at dusk sailed into Lanteen.

All the showboats had departed the town, save only *Fironzelle's Golden Conceit*. Tonight it glowed with a multitude of lights, as Garth Ashgale played an entertainment before a large audience. Rancor rose in Zamp's throat sour as bile. He hunched down on the seat. Useless now to curse or revile, but someday the tables would be turned!

The boats tied up to the dock; the bedraggled company clambered ashore and stood uncertainly, looking to Zamp for guidance.

Zamp spoke in a dispirited voice: "We must go our own ways. I am a ruined man; I can offer neither advice nor encouragement, except to suggest that all make their way to Coble by the best means possible and perhaps someday we will again sail the Vissel. The troupe is now dissolved."

"Where do you go?"

Zamp turned away. Damsel Blanche-Aster stood waiting for him. Zamp heaved a melancholy sigh. Could it be that his adversity had aroused a pang of sympathy within her chilly bosom? If so, Zamp was in the mood to be comforted. He took up her bundle of belongings. "Where do you wish to go?"

Zamp considered. "The Green Star Inn at the end of the esplanade is a roisterers' hangout, but inexpensive. It will serve my present purposes."

"It will serve mine as well."

Zamp, at this most dismal hour of his life, felt a glimmer of cheer. He said delicately, "I have salvaged a few valuables from the ruins: enough to see us to Coble, and I am more than willing to share with you."

"I have funds sufficient for my needs."

Zamp shrugged and blew out his cheeks. She was a skittish one for certain.

They set out along the esplanade. As they passed The Jolly Glassblower an enticing odor of barbecued meat came forth to tantalize them. Unfortunately, The Jolly Glassblower sold its food dear; at the Green Star Inn a bowl of stew with a crust and a draught of swamp-root beer could be had for a tenth the cost.

The esplanade ended; a walkway supported on crooked stilts led across tide* flats to the Green Star Inn, an erratic structure built of old planks, driftwood, warped bottles from the glassworks. On the verandah four men sat with their feet on the railing, drinking beer and indulging in coarse talk. They became silent as Zamp and Damsel Blanche-Aster, crossing the veranda, entered the inn, then fell to muttering to each other.

The common room spread wide under an irregular ceiling supported on equally eccentric posts. Lamps in the shape of green stars cast a sickly glow over tables where sat a number of undistinguished folk out for an evening's entertainment, while in a corner a rather slatternly woman pumped doleful music out of a concertina.

Zamp approached the bar and signaled to the innkeeper. "We require lodging at least for the night, together with a substantial meal, to be served as soon as possible."

"Very good, sir; our choicest room is luckily vacant. And aren't you Apollon Zamp of the famous showboat?"

"I am Zamp indeed."

The innkeeper came forth from behind the bar. "Along this hall, sir and madame; your room overlooks the river."

The room appeared comfortable enough, with a floor of reed mats, a mattress stuffed with tinselweed fluff and a table supporting a ewer of water. An adjacent privy overhung the mud-flats.

Zamp dropped Damsel Blanche-Aster's bundle upon the mattress; it fell apart and those garments she had elected to rescue tumbled forth, including an embroi-

---

*Solar tides; Big Planet lacks a moon.

dered blue jacket of great richness which Zamp had never seen her wear.

The innkeeper asked: "Will this do, sir?"

"Well enough," said Zamp. "We will be out for our supper in five minutes."

The innkeeper departed; Zamp turned to find Damsel Blanche-Aster staring at him. "You do not propose that we share this room?"

Zamp inspected the room. "It appears clean and comfortable; why not?"

Damsel Blanche-Aster said frigidly, "I do not wish to share any room whatever with you."

Zamp's disposition had been seriously abraded by events. He flung his hat to the floor, picked up her bundle and thrust it into her arms. "Find your own room. I am bored with your fastidiousness. Go your way and trouble me no further!"

Damsel Blanche-Aster marched to the door, opened it, then hesitated. She bowed her head and Zamp saw tears. Zamp's irascibility was usually short-lived; now he maintained a sullen silence. He could not forever be dancing this way and that like a puppet.

Damsel Blanche-Aster turned back into the room and put her bundle on the floor; she seemed wistful and young and tired to the point of exhaustion. Zamp went forward, took her bundle, set it on a chair, then clasped her in his arms, and despite her horrified expression found her mouth and kissed her. She made neither response nor resistance; Zamp might have been kissing a doll. He stood back in frustration.

Damsel Blanche-Aster wiped her mouth and finally found words. "Apollon Zamp, I wish to accompany you to Mornune, this is true. But I had hoped that you might curb your lust, or at least focus it upon some person or creature other than myself. I am faced with a dilemma. I do not care to sacrifice either my goals or what you call my fastidiousness.''

Zamp threw his hands in the air and walked back and forth across the room on long, bent-kneed strides. He cried: ''Your qualms are frustrating! Am I so ill-favored? Does blood course in your veins, or vinegar? Is life so long that we can afford to postpone a single pleasure?'' He went close to her and put his arms around her waist. ''Do you not feel a quickening of the pulse, a warmth in some inner region, a delightful weakness in your limbs?''

''I feel only hunger, fatigue and apathy.''

Zamp dropped his arms in disgust. ''No one can claim of Apollon Zamp that he coerced a woman against her will! However, I do not intend to vacate this room. Share it with me, or find another, at your option.''

''You may have the mattress. I will sleep on the floor.''

''Whatever you like. Meanwhile, let us wash our hands and then take our supper.''

Returning to the common room, they found that most of the old troupe had also arrived at the Green Star Inn and were negotiating for lodging and meals with the innkeeper.

Supper had been laid for Zamp and Damsel Blanche-Aster: bowls of thick soup, a platter of roasted larks, a pungent stew of herbs, clams and fish, a loaf of pollen-bread—a meal somewhat more lavish than Zamp had expected but to which he and Damsel Blanche-Aster did full justice. As he ate Zamp expressed his bewilderment and disappointment to Damsel Blanche-Aster. ''I am not a man who ordinarily allows emotion to interfere with his intellect; still your conduct distracts me from sober calculation—''

A hulking shape loomed over the table; it was Ulfimer,

captain of the grotesques. "You who claimed poverty and could not pay my salary: here you sit devouring larks while I must sell my boots to buy a dish or two of porridge! Do you wonder at my acrimony?"

"This is illogical!" declared Zamp heatedly. "You begrudge me a meal—I who lost vessel, iron and all? What have you lost? Only the wage you earned by allowing your appearance to disgust all onlookers."

"Do not belittle my abilities!" growled Ulfimer. "Whatever the case, you sit with grease on your chin while I bend double with hunger."

"In due course all will be set right," said Zamp. Ulfimer hunched away and Zamp once more turned his attention to Damsel Blanche-Aster. "I feel that you mistake the nature of my ardor. I propose, not a sordid little amour, but—"

Again he was interrupted, this time by the mime-girl, Lael-Rosaza, who glanced angrily sidewise at Damsel Blanche-Aster as she spoke. "Apollon Zamp, I can no longer restrain my bitterness! You have misused each mime-girl in turn, and what have we gained by such service? Nothing. Here you sit with your new woman, while I and Krissa and Demel and Septine must sell ourselves along the esplanade in order to exist!"

With an effort Zamp replied in an even voice, "Your language does you no credit. In due course I will command a new vessel, and I plan to rehire all the loyal members of my old troupe."

Lael-Rosza, paying no heed, had marched away.

Zamp heaved a weary sigh. "At the moment my fortunes are at a low ebb," he told Damsel Blanche-Aster. "They can only ascend. Meanwhile I desperately need your faith and affection. Believe me, we will share the rewards! Meanwhile, tonight for instance, is it too much to ask that—"

Again someone came to stand over their table; Zamp looked up to see Garth Ashgale. "Aha there, Zamp! I have heard the news of your mishap. My condolences! The catastrophe is felt by all of us!"

"I am despondent," said Zamp, "but not discouraged. I start afresh. Eventually I will reward my friends and punish my enemies. In a certain sense that wicked person who arranged my misadventure has done me a service, but still he will find no mercy."

"Ha, ha, Zamp, very good! I am pleased that events have not conquered your spirit!" He glanced down at Damsel Blanche-Aster in obvious curiosity, but Zamp performed no introductions. Ashgale spoke reflectively, "What of that affair up the river at Mornune?"

Zamp grunted. "King Waldemar can amuse himself by counting his toes, for all of me."

Damsel Blanche-Aster raised her eyes; meeting her blue gaze, Zamp said, "Nothing has yet been decided. We may still undertake the journey."

"In the pinnaces which brought you to Lanteen?"

"At Coble affairs will order themselves."

Ashgale could no longer contain his curiosity. "And this charming lady, what of her?"

"She is a member of my troupe."

"Indeed!" Ashgale addressed himself to Damsel Blanche-Aster. "May I enquire your specialties?"

Damsel Blanche-Aster made an airy gesture. "I am highly versatile. I sing in two voices; I wrestle bearded champions; I train oels to dance the mazurka."

"Remarkable!" declared Ashgale. "Since Zamp no longer owns a boat, would you care to transfer your capabilities to my vessel?"

"I am content as I am."

Ashgale made a suave gesture, then looked across the room to where the members of Zamp's old troupe sat over their gruel. Ashgale signaled the innkeeper. "At my expense, set before those excellent folk the fare they deserve. Are there more of those larks? Bring them forth, with trenchers of goulash and two dozen white cheese pasties."

"Bravo!" cried Viliweg. "Master Ashgale is a true nobleman!"

"My generosity is not entirely unpremeditated," said Ashgale. "I have decided to augment my programs with material of a frivolous nature, and I will consider hiring any qualified artists who are currently at liberty."

"Hurrah for Master Ashgale!" cried Alpo the acrobat.

Ashgale bowed and again signaled the innkeeper. "Serve flasks of medium-quality wine to my friends." Once again Ashgale was cheered. He held up his hand for silence. "I will not intrude upon your meal. Tonight relax and rest; tomorrow I will interview you aboard *Fironzelle's Golden Conceit*." He slapped clinking iron coins into the innkeeper's palm, bowed serenely to Damsel Blanche-Aster and departed the tavern.

Zamp immediately rose to his feet and went to address his former troupe. "Do not be fooled by Ashgale! The opportunities he offers are worthless!"

Viliweg uttered a jeering laugh. "Can you offer better?"

"The question is sterile," said Zamp. "However I will say this: when the new *Miraldra's Enchantment* floats the river, you may well regret deserting Apollon Zamp for the silken reptile who just departed the premises."

"We will salve those aches as we become aware of them!" retorted Alpo the acrobat, to stimulate an outburst of merriment from his fellows. Viliweg, in his exuberance, bestowed a gratuity upon the fat woman in the gown of black beads, and she played her concertina with even greater gusto.

Zamp leaned across the table and addressed himself to Damsel Blanche-Aster. "In this den of ruffians, conversation is impossible. Let us go out upon the veranda, or perhaps you would care to walk up and down the esplanade?"

Damsel Blanche-Aster said in a voice abstracted and somewhat listless: "I do not care for conversation. But sleep is impossible amid so much din."

Zamp rose to his feet and with a flourish which belied his own fatigue drew back her chair and helped her to arise. "We will go to sit out upon the veranda."

The innkeeper appeared at his elbow. "I have prepared your reckoning, Master Zamp."

Zamp stared in bewilderment. "My reckoning? I will settle my account when I leave the premises."

"There has been a mistake. Viliweg had already reserved the chamber into which I mistakenly placed you."

Zamp lowered his hand to the pommel of his rapier. "Three options are open for your consideration. You may return to Viliweg that sum double your ordinary rent which he has just paid you; you may arrange for me free and without charge the best room available at The Jolly Glassblower; or you may elect to spill a quantity of your red blood upon this floor."

The innkeeper drew back a step. "Your imputations are insulting! I am not a man to take kindly to threats! Still, as I now reflect upon the matter, the accommodation I promised Viliweg was not 'River Vista' which you occupy, but a section of the 'Placid Repose' dormitory overlooking the tide-flats. All is well, after all."

"Very good," said Zamp. "I trust there will be no further mistakes."

As they walked toward the door, Zamp was jostled by Viliweg the magician on his way to the bar. Viliweg said in a sharp voice, "Please be more careful; just now you trod upon my foot."

"Hold your tongue, Viliweg," said Zamp, more dispirited than annoyed. "Your complaints do not impress me."

Viliweg gave him a haughty glance, then turned away; Zamp and Damsel Blanche-Aster proceeded out upon the veranda. They seated themselves as far as possible from the group of glassblowers who still sat drinking beer and enjoying the evening air. Before them the great river Lant flowed deep and quiet toward its junction with the Vissel; on the far bank shone a few flickering yellow lamps. Aboard *Fironzelle's Golden Conceit* only the masthead lamp and the thief-takers still burned; but the light along the esplanade from the various booths and taverns made a vivacious show. Walls, talk and laughter reduced the wheezing of the concertina to a not-unpleasant undertone. Zamp inquired, "Would you care for a cordial, or a glass of Dulcinato?"

Taking her silence for assent, he signaled the potboy who had just brought beer to the glassblowers. "Bring us two goblets of Ysander's Quality Cordial, cool but not iced."

The potboy shook his head. "We keep a tub of Blue Ruin and another of Mutiny Rum; take your choice."

"Bring us a flask of good wine," said Zamp. He leaned back in his chair. "Back to our conversation—"

"I would prefer to sit in quiet."

Zamp gripped the arms of his chair. "But there is so much to discuss! I know absolutely nothing about you, other than that you are both lovely and proud."

"I do not care to discuss myself."

"Tell me one thing," Zamp insisted. "Are you espoused, or betrothed or faithful to some far lover? Is this the reason for your behavior?"

"None of these."

"So then, you find me repulsive?"

Damsel Blanche-Aster focused her eyes upon Zamp. "If we must talk, let it be to practical ends. First, how do you propose to gain control of another boat?"

"When we reach Coble, we shall see."

"And how long might be required to prepare such a boat for a voyage up the Vissel?"

Zamp shrugged. "A dozen factors are involved. If I owned my five pounds of iron, no more than a week or two. But I am curious to know why you are so anxious to reach Mornune."

"There is no mystery. Whoever wins Waldemar's competition earns a palace and great wealth. I wish to espouse such a man and live the life of a princess."

Zamp gave his head a marveling shake and poured the wine which the potboy had served. "You have calculated the course of your life with meticulous care."

"Why should I not? Have I any other life?"

"I hold no fixed beliefs," said Zamp, "Much has been said, up one side and down another; the question remains open. Still, folk who plot their lives with too exact a precision often miss the fascinating twists and byways of a more picturesque route, ultimately to the same destination."

"How long until we can arrive at Coble?"

"Before long one vessel or another will depart Lanteen down-river. We will take passage aboard."

"What of the fare? Can you pay?"

"Certainly! I salvaged all my jewels, which command considerable value." And Zamp struck the pocket of his jacket, only to find it flat. He sat up in his chair. "I have been robbed! How did it occur?" He jerked around and gazed toward the door. "When Viliweg jostled me, he made a set of confusing gestures. The jewels are now gone!"

"What of the silver plaque?"

Zamp touched an inner pocket. "It is safe."

"Let me see it."

Zamp brought forth the glittering tablet. Damsel Blanche-Aster took it into her hand and gave a grateful sigh. "It is the same."

Zamp retrieved the tablet and restored it to his pocket. "It is also my last resource. I must use it to pay for our bed and board."

Damsel Blanche-Aster shook her head. "I will pay the innkeeper. I will also secure our passage to Coble."

Zamp looked at her in surprise. "I had no idea that you carried so much iron!"

Damsel Blanche-Aster ignored the remark. "We can now arrange matters on a businesslike footing. I can expedite our journey to Coble, but I insist that you exclude me from your erotic fantasies."

"Bah," grunted Zamp. "What if I choose to throw the plaque in the river?"

"I could not prevent you."

"You could dissuade me."

Damsel Blanche-Aster made no reply. Zamp brought forth the plaque and held it in his hand, hefting it thoughtfully. Damsel Blanche-Aster rose to her feet and went into the tavern, presumably to her bed in "River Vista."

Zamp clenched his teeth and looked up at the sky. He replaced the plaque in his pocket and sat alone in the darkness.

Within, the sounds or revelry waxed and waned. Viliweg came reeling through the door and went to stand by the rail. Zamp, approaching quietly seized the magician about the legs and hurled him over the rail, down into the slime of the mud-flats.

Zamp went moodily to "River Vista." A lamp burnt low on the table. Damsel Blanche-Aster lay under her cloak in a corner of the room, her sleek blonde head pillowed on the embroidered jacket.

Zamp knew that she was not asleep. He said gruffly, "You may share the mattress without agonizing over the priceless sanctity of your body, which after all is much like any other. At this moment it means no more to me than the table."

Chapter 7

Coble, situated where the main channel of the Vissel entered Surmise Bay, was a town of tall, steep-gabled buildings of timber and black brick, netted by a hundred canals, shaded by a thousand lordly halcositic dendrons, along with innumerable lantans, palms and plume willows. The business of Coble centered on the Burse, a small square overlooked by crooked old buildings, the windows tinted purple and green with age. A hundred yards east flowed the Vissel River, and here at Bynum's Dock was moored the *Universal Pancomium*, a floating museum owned by Throdorus Gassoon. The *Universal Pancomium* had never been reckoned a beautiful vessel, being somewhat spare and gaunt of outline, with a stern paddle-wheel powered by eighteen bullocks at three capstans, in addition to the sails which Gassoon used only under optimum conditions.

Gassoon was as spare, gaunt and graceless as his boat. His face was long and pale, his eyes were pale, small and close beside his long equine nose; his hair was an unruly shock of white tufts. He habitually wore a tight and threadbare suit of black twill with black stockings and black shoes, in unkind contrast to his pale skin and white hair. His arms and legs were lank; he walked at a lope; halting, he tended to throw his long face back like a neighing horse.

Gassoon had few friends; he devoted all his time, love and attention to the curios, relicts and oddities of his collection. Travelers from afar marveled at the *Universal Pancomium*; never had they seen the match of Gassoon's remarkable exhibits. His cases displayed the most diverse objects: costumes from far regions of Big Planet; weapons and musical instruments; models of spaceships and aircraft; dioramas of fabulous scenes; maps and globes of various inhabited worlds; photographs, books and art reproductions of Earthly provenance brought to Big Planet during the original immigrations; a periodic table with glass vials containing samples of each element; a collection of minerals and crystals; a toy steam engine built of brass, which Gassoon sometimes operated to amuse the children.

Twice a year, during those intervals between the monsoons, when the air hung still and heavy, he took the *Universal Pancomium* out on the river and performed a cautious circuit of the delta towns, sometimes venturing up the Vissel as far as Wigtown, or even Ratwick, and once, throwing caution to the winds, he had voyaged to Badburg. As much as possible he traveled on the thrust of his stern-wheel. Sailing made him uneasy; he distrusted the whims of awesome and uncontrollable forces out of the sky, and was truly comfortable only when moored snug up against Bynum's Dock.

Aboard the *Universal Pancomium* came all sorts of folk, of every race and gradation of caste. Gassoon reckoned himself as expert at identifying and classifying these folks as a man could be. He also had an appreciative eye for beautiful women, and his interest, therefore, was doubly stimulated one afternoon by the sight of a slim young woman in a gray cloak, whose erect carriage suggested aristocracy, but whose racial background was not immediately evident. Gassoon approved of her coolness and poise, her sleek blonde hair, the delightful modeling of her features. Gassoon often indulged himself in grand daydreams, wherein he conquered empires, founded noble cities and made the name Throdorus Gassoon revered across the lunes of Big Planet. This particular young woman might have stepped out of one of these daydreams, so clear-eyed and romantically pensive was she, so charged with an indefinable élan.

Definitely a most interesting young woman. Gassoon considered her features, her garments, her posture as she wandered among his exhibits. She showed interest in his maps, charts and globes, which pleased Gassoon; here was no vulgar little hussy to coo and gurgle over trinkets and gewgaws.

Gassoon, for all his lore, subscribed to a common fallacy: he assumed that all those whom he encountered appraised him in the same terms as he did himself. To Gassoon his tight black suit signified elegant simplicity. When he saw his pallid, long-nosed face with its wild brush of white hair in the mirror, he saw the face of a defiant Prometheus, a visionary aesthete. Musing among his relics, Gassoon had loved, suffered, gloried, despaired; he had known the surge and crash of empires; he had listened to titanic musics; he had roamed far space. A single glance must convey to a sensitive mind the wondrous richness which Gassoon carried behind the noble jut of his forehead.

Therefore, without modesty or diffidence, he approached the young woman in the gray cloak. "I see that you are interested in maps. I approve of this. Maps nurture the imagination, enrich the soul."

The young woman appraised him with candid interest. Gassoon approved her self-possession: no titters, no simpering, no insipid confessions of utter ignorance. She asked, "Are you the proprietor of this ship?"

"Yes, I am Throdorus Gassoon. Do you find my exhibits worthy of note?"

The young woman nodded rather absently. "Your exhibits are most interesting. I would think that they are unique in Lune XXIII."

"And elsewhere! Have you never before heard of the *Universal Pancomium*?"

"Never."

"Ha ha! At least you are frank. And where, may I ask, is your home?"

The young woman stared absently at the map. "At the moment I am staying here in Coble. Do you often take your vessel to distant places?"

"From time to time. I have visited Ratwick and Wigtown at the mouth of the Murne, and I frequently cruise the waters of the delta."

"You are, in a sense, a benefactor for all the folk who otherwise might never see these things."

Gassoon gave a modest wave of his big white hand. "This might be true. I never think of myself in such terms; I enjoy my work. I like showing people my collection. Come along over here, notice in this cabinet: the skeleton of a fossil oel! And this is the trance-mask of a Kalkar shaman! And here are silver coins from the Earthly Middle Ages; they were antiques even when brought here to Big Planet!"

"Remarkable! Of all the showboats this is truly the finest!"

Gassoon raised his eyebrows. " 'Showboats'? Well, why not? I refuse to recoil at a word."

"You evidently disapprove of the other showboats?"

Gassoon pursed his lips. "No doubt they serve their purpose."

"At Lanteen I witnessed productions aboard *Miraldra's Enchantment* and *Fironzelle's Golden Conceit*. Both were elaborate and carefully staged."

"Quite so. Still, on either boat did you discern any scintilla of intellectual content? No? I thought not. Apollon Zamp is a popinjay, Ashgale a poseur; their audiences leave no better than when they arrived. Is it any wonder why many folk along the Vissel are semi-barbarous?"

"You would seem to believe that showboats might serve a more constructive function."

"That goes without saying. Consider the human mind! It is capable of amazing feats when used properly. Conversely, without exercise it atrophies to a lump of gray-yellow fat. But why not come to my office, where we can continue our chat in comfort?"

"With pleasure."

Gassoon made no apology for the disorder of his office which was cluttered with papers, folios, books, crates, oddments of this and that, as well as a table and two leather chairs which, through some deficiency in the tanning process, had never ceased to exude an unpleasant odor.

Gassoon cleared off one of the chairs. "Be seated if you please. Will you take a cup of tea? Excuse me while I notify my factotum." Gassoon stepped out of the office and called down a companionway. "Berard, are you there? Be so good as to reply when I call! Prepare a pot of fresh tea and bring it to the office. Use the preparation in the red jar."

Gassoon reurned to find Damsel Blanche-Aster inspecting a pamphlet she had picked up from the table. Gassoon seated himself, hitched forward his chair and clasped his hands across his chest. "I see that you are interested in botany?"

"To some extent. I don't pretend to understand this."

"It is written in the dialect of Cusp XIX North. How it found its way to Coble across three oceans and two continents is beyond conjecture. The author discusses the accommodation of native flora to imports from Earth, and cites a number of fascinating instances. The exotic organisms, he discovers, after a period of utter triumph or absolute defeat seem to 'make their peace with the world,' as he puts it, then across the centuries gradually converge toward the native types. In his epilogue, he wonders if the same may be true of humanity? And he indicates a number of peoples: the Goads of Passaway Valley, the Rhute Long-necks, the Padraic Mountain Darklings, where the process is already much advanced."

"I have never heard of these places, or these peoples," said Damsel Blanche Aster demurely.

"I will point them out on my maps," declared Gassoon with enthusiasm.

Berard the steward shuffled into the office with a tray; he dropped it upon the table, sniffed, and departed. Gassoon snapped his fingers in happy anticipation of the treat and poured tea into a pair of black stoneware mugs. He looked up under arched eyebrows. "By the way, whom do I have the pleasure of entertaining?"

"Damsel Blanche-Aster Wittendore is the useful part of my name." She returned the pamphlet to the table. "I am very impressed by your ambition to inform and enlighten the folk of the Great Vissel Basin. It seems most courageous and idealistic."

Gassoon blinked. Had he asserted so large a purpose? Even if not, it was pleasant to feel the approval of this handsome and intelligent young woman. "For a fact, the project has never been attempted; but then very few persons are qualified to direct such a program."

"How, exactly, will you proceed? I presume that you plan to use your remarkable boat as a base of operations."

Gassoon leaned back in his chair and stared up at the ceiling. "In all candor, I have arrived at no definite decisions."

"Oh! I am sorry to hear this!"

Gassoon made a tent with his fingers and frowned thoughtfully. "The project is not all that simple. I am certain that folk everywhere would prefer entertainment which concedes the dignity of their intellect to the meretricious trash foisted on them by the usual show-boat. They flock aboard these craft merely because nothing better is offered."

"I am sure that this is true," said Damsel Blanche-Aster. "What kind of program might you offer?"

Gassoon startled her by pounding his fist down on the table. He spoke in a ringing voice: "The classics, of course! The works of the Earthly masters!" Then, as if abashed by his own vehemence, he took up his tea and sipped.

Damsel Blanche-Aster presently said, "I am ashamed that I know so little of these things."

Gassoon laughed. "I dream too largely. My schemes are impractical."

"You do yourself injustice," said Damsel Blanche-Aster in a soft voice. "Folk everywhere recognize sincerity, no matter in what guise it appears. Personally, I am bored with callow ideas and callow people."

"Your feelings do you credit," said Gassoon. "Beyond question you are a person of discernment. Still, all balanced against all, the works to which I refer make demands of those who would appreciate them. The metaphors sometimes span two or three abstractions; the perorations are addressed to unknown agencies, the language is archaic and ambiguous. . . . In spite of all, the works exhale a peculiar fervor." Gassoon leaned back in his chair and tossed his white mane fretfully askew. "I ask myself questions which have no answers. Is art absolute? Or is it a plane cutting across a civilization at a certain point in time? Perhaps fundamentally I am asking: does aesthetic perception arrive through the mind or through the heart? As you must have decided, I am inclined to the romantic view—still, sophisticated art demands a sophisticated audience; so much must be assumed."

Damsel Blanche-Aster sipped from the earthenware mug. "A remarkable thought has entered my mind . . . perhaps I should not mention it; you would think me forward."

"Suggest by all means!" declared Gassoon. "I find your interest most heart-warming."

"What I will tell you so strangely meshes with your ambitions as to suggest the workings of Destiny. You know of King Waldemar's festival at Mornune?"

"I have heard something of the event."

"I arrived at Coble yesterday aboard a riverboat. Also aboard was Apollon Zamp, the former master of *Miraldra's Enchantment*."

" 'Former' master?"

"Yes; he lost his ship at Port Whant. But first he had earned an invitation from King Waldemar to the Mornune festival. So then: why should you not sail to Mornune in his place and perform before King Waldemar? I would consider myself privileged if you would allow me to sail with you!"

Gassoon blinked and pulled dubiously at his chin. "The way is very long."

Damsel Blanche-Aster laughed. "Such a consideration should never deter a man like yourself."

"But is the project feasible?" asked Gassoon rather plaintively. "After all, Zamp has the summons, not I."

Damsel Blanche-Aster said positively, "Zamp will cooperate, because of the grand prize." She leaned forward and looked Gassoon full in the face. "Is it not a wonderful adventure?"

"Yes indeed," Croaked Gassoon, "but I am not an adventurous man."

"This I cannot believe! I sense in you a romantic zest which transcends age!"

Gassoon jerked at the lapels of his coat. "I am not after all so old."

"Of course not. A man is only old when he abandons his dreams."

"Never!" cried Gassoon. "Never!"

Damsel Blanche-Aster smiled gently. "I have some slight acquaintance with Apollon Zamp. I can bring him here and something remarkable must eventuate out of all this." She rose to her feet.

Gassoon leapt erect. "Must you go so soon? I will order up fresh tea!"

"I must go to find Apollon Zamp! You have aroused hope and enthusiasm in me, Throdorus Gassoon!"

"Go," said Gassoon in a full voice. "But return soon."

"As soon as possible."

Leaving the ship, Damsel Blanche-Aster walked slowly along Bynum's Dock, head bowed pensively; a person softer and more melancholy than either Apollon Zamp or Throdorus Gassoon might have reckoned. She halted to look back at the *Universal Pancomium*. After a moment she winced slightly with an emotion she could not have defined to herself. Turning once more, she passed under an arch and into a crooked little way which slanted this way and that between tall structures of time-darkened wood. By a humpbacked bridge she crossed a canal of black-green water. Ahead a building of a dozen eccentric dormers straddled the way; to one side of the passage underneath was an herbalist's shop, to the other a small bookbindery. Damsel Blanche-Aster passed through and out into the Burse, a square not as wide as the surrounding buildings were high. At the center, where four flower vendors had set up their booths, Zamp was to have met her, but he was nowhere to be seen. Damsel Blanche-Aster showed neither surprise nor vexation. Surveying the square, she noticed a sign suspended over the cobbles, displaying the emblem of a blue fish; Damsel Blanche-Aster turned her steps in this direction.

The dark interior of the Blue Narwhal, like other establishments fronting the Burse, conducted its business in rather cramped quarters. Zamp sat at a small table on a dais in the bay window; at her approach he sprang gallantly to his feet.

Damsel Blanche-Aster allowed herself to be seated, and composed her face into that indifferent mask which she deemed most useful for her dealings with Zamp.

"I have just come from the *Universal Pancomium*," she told him. "There I met Throdorus Gassoon. I mentioned your circumstances, and he saw fit to make a constructive suggestion. He is willing to take his vessel to Mornune and participate in the festival. His boat will necessarily be known as *Miraldra's Enchantment*, and you will be the ostensible master."

Zamp scowled. "I have met Gassoon before. He is as dull as a stump, and opinionated to boot."

"He has definite ideas, this is true. In fact, he refuses to present the frivolities and pastiches such as those which won you your reputation."

Zamp was more surprised than annoyed. "What then does he have in mind?"

"He wants to play the classic dramas of ancient Earth."

Zamp made a weary gesture. "I am no pedant; what do I know of such things?"

"No more than I. But you have the talent to vitalize any material."

"I have not yet vitalized you."

"First you must vitalize yourself and Gassoon's antique epics."

"And then?"

Damsel Blanche-Aster shrugged. "Whoever pleases King Waldemar at the festival earns himself a fortune. You can build the grandest vessel ever to sail the river, or you can remain at Mornune and live the life of a grandee."

Zamp sat inspecting her with unflattering objectivity. She bore the scrutiny a moment, then became uncomfortable. "I told Gassoon that you would arrive shortly to make your arrangements with him."

Zamp paused a suspenseful moment, then rose to his feet. "I can lose nothing."

They departed the Blue Narwhal Tavern, crossed the Burse, and walked by the crooked way to Bynum's Dock. Here Damsel Blanche-Aster halted. "I will go no farther. It is not wise that Gassoon should see us together. Now please listen. Gassoon must not be antagonized. Dispute none of his theories; concede as much as you can. Above all, don't quarrel about authority; Gassoon must believe that he is in charge of the expedition. Right now time is short, and our objective is to get under way."

"This is undoubtedly your objective," grumbled Zamp. "It is not necessarily mine."

"Oh? Where are we at odds?"

"I do not care to make a fool of myself at Mornune. If Gassoon insists on some impossible nonsense, why should I waste time and energy just to pull your chestnuts out of the fire? You have made it quite clear that you detest me."

"No, no, no!" cried Damsel Blanche-Aster. "I detest no one, not even you! But I can make no personal commitments—not now."

"Nor ever."

Damsel Blanche-Aster's eyes sparkled. "Why do you say that? Because your sulks and vanities and foppish habits leave me cold? Look at you with your blonde curls, your airs and graces, your ridiculous hats!" She stamped her foot. "Once and for all make up your mind! If you win at Mornune, you gain wealth, and this is your prize—not my admiration, which you may or may not gain!"

Zamp laughed in her face. "One thing is certain: your understanding of me is as small and dim as is mine of you. Very well, admire me or not; I don't care. As you point out, the prize at Mornune is iron, and I am the man to gain it." He turned away and surveyed the *Universal Pancomium*. "Throdorus Gassoon, here I come. Prepare yourself for the experience of your life."

Damsel Blanche-Aster reached out and touched his arm. "Apollon Zamp."

Zamp looked over his shoulder. "Yes?"

"Do your best."

Zamp nodded curtly and sauntered off toward the *Universal Pancomium*. He climbed the gangway and halted at the wicket where Berard the factotum presently showed his face. "Admission is half a groat, sir."

"Half a groat be damned. I am Apollon Zamp! Inform Throdorus Gassoon that I have come to call."

"Step this way, sir; Master Gassoon is at his calisthenics and for still another five minutes cannot be disturbed."

"I will wait."

Zamp strolled about the exhibits and presently Gassoon appeared. "Ah, Zamp! A pleasure to see you! I notice that you are studying the maps!"

"Yes; the Bottomless Lake exerts its fascination."

"For me as well. Shall we repair to my office?"

Zamp seated himself in the chair Damsel Blanche-Aster had occupied only two hours earlier. Gassoon poured out two tots of Brio. "Allow me to express my sympathy in regard to the loss of your boat."

"Thank you. The disaster of course was my own fault; I trusted that scoundrel Garth Ashgale. Still, I know how to earn iron for another boat, which is what brings me here." Zamp produced the silver plaque and placed it in front of Gassoon. "Whoever succeeds in amusing King Waldemar wins a fortune."

"So what is your proposal?"

"That we temporarily change the name of your vessel to *Miraldra's Enchantment*, that we hire a troupe, then sail up the Vissel to Mornune and compete for the grand prize."

Gassoon nodded slowly. "About as I expected—and mind you, not an unreasonable proposition. But I am not a man for flamboyance or notoriety and I already have more iron than I care to spend. Zamp, I have larger ambitions! Today I fell into conversation with a most charming young lady, Damsel Blanche-Aster, and she left me in a peculiar mood. I see that my life has been somewhat stagnant, even self-centered. I have gloated privately over treasures of literature which should have been shared with others. Now I wish to produce and stage some famous masterpieces of ancient Earth.

You ask, where are these fabulous classics to be found? I reply, they are here with my collection of rare books, no fifty feet from where we sit.

"Most interesting," said Zamp. "Where does this take us?"

"To my own proposal, which is this: I shall select, with your wise counsel, one or more of these master-works, which we then will play at Mornune. If we win the prize, so be it! If we fail, at least we have the satisfaction of doing our utmost."

Zamp said, "I am not familiar with the classics you mention. For all I know they might prove a remarkable success! In principle I agree to your terms. But I must put forward some counter-terms. Several come to mind. For instance, since I am dedicated to winning the Mornune competition and you are not, I must arrange the nice details of production, including personnel, costumes, music and staging."

Gassoon made a nasal and reedy expostulation, with one white finger held high. "Always within the limits imposed by the original version!"

Zamp made a gesture of easy acquiescence. "Now as to the ship: we will naturally require a suitable stage and seating arrangements. A more festive appearance would not go amiss. A few touches of pink and green paint, three dozen banners and a hundred yards of bunting will work wonders for this stark old death-ship. Another matter: you are a proud and competent mariner and naturally will command your craft as we ply up-river—until we reach Bottomless Lake. Then is the time and place of my great concern, and I would wish to assume command until after our performance before King Waldemar."

"These requirements are not altogether unreasonable," said Gassoon. "However, I must make still other stipulations. I intend that Damsel Blanche-Aster should accompany us. A stage, as you say, must be constructed and seats provided; however, I do not propose to disrupt the arrangement of my museum.''

Zamp pursed his lips dubiously. "I fear that some small dislocation might be necessary, if only to accommodate the machinery of the stage. Additionally we must equip ourselves with double robber-nets and the usual precautions against nomad attack.''

Gassoon was obstinate in his refusal. "Quite unnecessary! Throughout history wandering minstrels, scholar-poets, bards, scops, druithines and troubadours—all are accorded safe passage across the most dangerous lands. Such is human tradition; why should it be otherwise on Big Planet?''

Zamp sipped the Brio, which, having sat too long in the bottle, had become musty. "These are noble ideals and do you credit; I wish that the nomads were as high-minded.''

Gassoon smiled and drank down his own Brio with relish. "Approach any man, no matter how base or ferocious, greet him with dignity and candor, and he will do you no wrong. The precautions you suggest are not only expensive, they are unnecessary. Peace is the word! Think peace! We come in peace and go in peace!''

Zamp gave a noncommittal nod. The matter could be deferred until later.

Gassoon cleared his throat and poured a few more drops of Brio into the cups. "I understand that you became acquainted with Damsel Blanche-Aster at Lanteen?''

"Quite true.''

"She seems a most remarkable person.''

"So she seems, indeed.''

"Where might be her place of origin?''

"She has never commented upon this matter. In fact, we have never discussed our personal affairs in any degree whatever."

Gassoon blew out his cheeks and stared off into space. "After so many years of placidity, I am suddenly quite excited."

"I as well." Zamp raised his cup. "To the success of our great adventure!"

"To success!" Gassoon tossed down the rank liquid with a flourish, and wiped his mouth. "We must discuss financial arrangements. How much iron can you contribute to the venture?"

Zamp stared across the table in shock. "I already have offered my expertise and the absolutely indispensable summons of King Waldemar! Do you expect iron as well?"

Gassoon's mouth, between the long nose and the long, pale chin, became almost invisible. He said at last, "Am I to understand that you can contribute no iron?"

"Not a groat."

"This is sour news indeed. The cost will be exorbitant."

"For a stage, a few scats, a bucket or two of paint? Hardly more than ordinary maintenance!"

"We must assemble a troupe," Gassoon insisted mulishly. "They will require certain sums from time to time."

"No problem there," replied Zamp bluffly. "I know precisely how to deal with such demands—namely, ignore them."

"These persons cannot be put off forever; they will become sulky."

"We will derive income from performances along the way; in no time all expenses will be reimbursed."

Gassoon was still not reassured. "Possibly so. Still, I had not intended to advance so large a sum."

Zamp threw up his hands in annoyance. "The project will then go by the boards, since I am penniless. Excuse me, I must notify the Damsel Blanche-Aster of your decision."

"Not so fast!" Gassoon squeezed shut his eyes and sat motionless a strained five seconds. In a bleak voice he said, "The matter is not all that significant. As you point out, casual performances must surely cover the expense."

Zamp resumed his seat. "Allow me to make a suggestion. The time of the Mornune Festival is not far in the future. Our preparations should begin instantly."

Gassoon leaned back and turned his eyes so far up to the ceiling that cusps of white showed below. Once again the entire venture quivered in the balance. He sighed. "I will meet you later in the day; we will discuss our plans in greater detail."

Zamp reported the events of the meeting to Damsel Blanche-Aster.

"So then," she said in a soft voice, half to herself, "the project is underway."

"I would think so. He may still change his mind."

Damsel Blanche-Aster shook her head slowly. "He will not change his mind."

"You don't seem exultant."

She shook her head. "I do what I must do."

"As always, your moods elude me," growled Zamp.

Damsel Blanche-Aster only asked, "Where do you next meet Master Gassoon, and when?"

"At the Mariner's Rest, when the sun hangs above Farewell Mountain."

"I shall be there."

Chapter 8

Zamp, for want of better entertainment, marched back and forth along the seawall, tossing pebbles out into Surmise Bay. To the west, the shoreline curved seaward, to end at the dark crag known as Farewell Mountain. As Zamp walked he carefully gauged the descent of Phaedra, and in due course posted himself where he could watch along the quay.

Precisely at the appointed hour he observed Gassoon approaching and stepped smartly forward; the two met in front of the Mariner's Rest.

"You are punctual," said Gassoon. "It is a virtue I appreciate."

"I return the compliment," said Zamp. "I believe that we have arrived exactly at the same instant."

"A happy omen." Gassoon led the way into the tavern and spoke a word to the proprietor, who ushered them into a small, private parlor, with a bow window overlooking the river. A lamp of three flames and eight lenses hung over a round table upon which Gassoon placed the leather case he had brought with him; Zamp meanwhile placed an order for sausages and beer with the innkeeper.

Gassoon settled himself into one of the chairs. "I have carefully considered our conversation." He paused a portentous moment. "Our goals are reconciled if, and only if, we totally agree upon the style and quality of our presentation."

"Certainly," said Zamp. "All this goes without saying."

Gassoon peevishly moved his portfolio to make room for the innkeeper's tray of beer and sausages. "My remark is really not so trite as it may seem. I wish to nip in the bud any thought of buffoonery, waggling of rumps, topical ballads sung in bogus dialects."

Zamp made an easy gesture. "Agreed, signed and certified."

Gassoon grunted and opened his portfolio. "This afternoon I looked through my collection and selected certain works which might be suitable for our purposes."

With his mouth full of sausage, Zamp reached for one of the volumes; Gassoon deftly moved it back out of Zamp's reach. He spoke in his reediest, most didactic voice. "The program which we have in mind presents formidable difficulties. The language has changed; conventions and symbols also change. Men as knowledgeable as ourselves will puzzle over some of the obscure allusions: how then for the folk of our audiences, who, no matter how earnest and keen, will still be unprepared?"

Zamp quaffed a hearty draught of beer, and setting down the mug, wiped his mouth with the back of his hand. "To these folk we usually present the vulgarisms which you deplore, and there is never any difficulty."

Gassoon ignored the remark. "We can either adapt and edit and to some extent alter the flavor of the original, or we can present the matter without compromise, and trust in the perceptivity of our audiences. What is your opinion?"

Zamp wiped his hands with the napkin. "Our basic

purpose is to win King Waldemar's approval; hence we must at least be intelligible."

Gassoon made a prim correction. "Our basic purpose is recreation of the classics. If King Waldemar is sensitive and subtle we will win the prize."

"In that case," said Zamp thoughtfully, "we should prepare several programs, to be ready for anything."

Gassoon's response was once again negative. "It would be pleasant to hire a large number of skillful performers and prepare an extensive repertory. Needless to say, I cannot afford to do this. We must settle upon one or two works which are not too costly to stage. For instance, here is a work known as *Macbeth*, which has long been considered a classic."

Zamp thumbed through the work with dubiously pursed lips. Gassoon watched him expressionlessly. Finally, Zamp said: "In my experience audiences prefer any kind of spectacle to verbiage. If we can augment certain of these scenes and truncate others, and all in all introduce a bit more color, we might have a feasible product."

Gassoon said mildly, "This work, in its present form, has stood the test of time. Don't forget, I plan to transcend the efforts of the ordinary showboats!"

In spite of his firm resolve, Zamp found himself arguing with Gassoon. "This is Big Planet, where eccentricities abound! What succeeds at one town, fails at another twenty miles along the river. At Skivaree on the Murne, the folk have a hysterical tendency; if once they are amused, they cannot stop laughing, and the wise shipmaster presents a program of religious tracts. At Henbane Berm, masculine roles must be played by females, and females by men; do not ask me why; they insist that dramas be performed in this way. Down-river towns such as Badburg, Port Moses, Port Optimo, Spanglemar, Ratwick, are somewhat easier; still each has its peculiarities, which are ignored at risk."

Gassoon raised his finger into the air. "You ignore the single essential element: the fact that all these folk are men. Their perceptions and instincts are basically alike; all—" A knock sounded at the door. Gassoon jumped up, opened the door a crack, peered forth, then threw the door wide. "Enter, by all means!"

Damsel Blanche-Aster came into the room. Gassoon brought forward a chair. "Please be seated. Will you take a glass of wine? Or one of these quite tolerable sausages? You will be interested in our conversation. We are debating aesthetic theory and find ourselves at loggerheads. I maintain that art is universal and eternal. Master Zamp—I hope that I fairly state his case—feels that local idiosyncrasies invalidate this precept."

Damsel Blanche-Aster said, "Perhaps both of you are right."

Gassoon knit his brows. "I concede that this is possible. So it becomes our mission to dissolve this stunted parochialism."

"I only want to win the Mornune competition," said Zamp gloomily.

"Understandable! Nevertheless we must focus on the main objective. It might be wiser to—"

Zamp sighed. "Unless we agree as to the Mornune Festival, our association ends almost before it starts."

"I would regret this," said Gassoon. "Still, you must do as you see fit. Damsel Blanche-Aster and I will pursue our own goals."

Damsel Blanche-Aster said, "In my opinion a victory at the Mornune Festival is extremely important, if only for the sake of prestige. In this instance I support Master Zamp."

Gassoon's face fell. "Such a victory no doubt would enhance our reputations," he said grudgingly. "Well then, I believe that we should settle upon the classic tragedy *Macbeth* as our basic vehicle."

Zamp opposed this concept. "What if King Waldemar detests tragedy? Suppose that he is highly partial to pastiches like those I presented on *Miraldra's Enchantment?* We should prepare two, or better, three programs. Include *Macbeth* if you must, but also let us have something with music and gaiety and merry spectacles."

"The matter of expense must curb any elaborate ambitions," declared Gassoon. "I am not the wealthiest man of Lune XXIII." He shuffled through his books. "Here is a musical work: *H.M.S. Pinafore*, which seems gay enough, though it is not particularly broad."

"That need not trouble us, so long as the work has popular appeal."

Gassoon sniffed and put *H.M.S. Pinafore* aside. "Here is an odd work: *The Critique of Pure Reason*, which evidently carries serious import."

Zamp glanced through the book. "It could not be presented except as a costumed allegory or a dithyramb."

"Now here is another work. . . ."

The discussion continued for another two hours, and eventually agreement was reached, both Zamp and Gassoon making concessions. Zamp was forced to abandon his program of gay miscellaneities, and Gassoon undertook to provide costumes and settings for *Macbeth* on a scale considerably more lavish than he had intended. Zamp privately considered the work too heavy and was resolved to introduce diversions and spectacles; Gassoon had satisfied himself that Zamp's tastes were vulgar and insensitive. Damsel Blanche-Aster showed small interest in the proceedings and studied the pictures in a tattered volume of *Paradise Lost*, which Zamp had wished to produce, but which Gassoon had rejected for reasons of excessive expenditure. Zamp was reluctantly granted control over production details, while Gassoon assumed responsibility for navigation. Gassoon was also conceded the office of adviser and monitor in regard to the production. "I will insist upon meticulous techniques," Gassoon declared. "We can't afford untidy execution. Every detail must be keen and bright as a diamond, every gesture must be rich with emotion; silence must carry a meaning heavier than words." Warming to his theme, Gassoon jumped to his feet and paced back and forth across the parlor. Damsel Blanche-Aster watched him as a hypnotized rabbit might watch a serpent, turning her head back and forth.

Zamp lost interest in Gassoon's remarks and examined *Macbeth* in greater detail. He was forced to admit that the work projected a weird, unreal emotion which he thought he might be able to capture and recreate, with a few modifications and augmentations of his own.

Gassoon stopped in mid-stride, to frown down at Zamp. "I trust that these seven stipulations, or more accurately, strictures of interpretation, accord with your own point of view?"

"Your ideas certainly have merit," said Zamp absently. "I notice, incidentally, that the musical accompaniment is missing."

Gassoon peered down at the ancient volume. "It is so indeed! A pity."

"No great matter; the concertmaster will provide a suitable score."

"Concertmaster? Is such a functionary essential?"

Zamp gave a quizzical shrug. "No one is absolutely essential. A concertmaster will release me from the responsibility of rehearsing the musicians."

"The most competent of the musicians can take on this work," Gassoon decided. "Or if necessary, I will do so myself—anything to avoid useless expense."

"That idea, at least, has merit, and to this end, rather

than waste money at an inn, I will take up residence on the new *Miraldra's Enchantment*, as it now must be known.''

Gassoon reluctantly agreed to this proposal. Damsel Blanche-Aster said softly, ''Perhaps there is an area of responsibility I might assume?''

''A generous thought,'' declared Gassoon. ''Still—''

''Damsel Blanche-Aster might supervise the steward's department,'' suggested Zamp. ''The quality of the victualing, the comfort of the cabins, dormitories, saloons and other such amenities.''

''This task had better be left to me,'' Gassoon decided. ''I am an old hand at arranging economies. But why should not the Damsel Blanche-Aster play a part in the drama? Why not Lady Macbeth herself?''

''An excellent idea,'' said Zamp.

Damsel Blanche-Aster made no objection. ''I will do my best.''

''Tomorrow, then,'' said Zamp, ''I will set about the task of assembling a troupe. I will naturally require an expense account.''

Only after twenty minutes of heated discussion was the matter resolved, to the full satisfaction of neither Zamp, who enjoyed good living, nor Gassoon, who disliked paying for Zamp's self-indulgences. As they left the Mariner's Rest, Gassoon was further annoyed when he was presented the bill for Zamp's beer and sausages.

Chapter 9

At a dock near the Burse, Zamp hired a green punt with a green-and-white-striped awning and was conveyed along the waterways of Coble; under four-storied structures of dark timber, beside moored houseboats, under overhanging plum willows and stern black lantans. At Tasselmyer's Dock Zamp alighted and walked along the Street of Sounds, beside the small shops where musical instruments were fabricated for export across Surmise Bay to Leuland, and much of Lune XXIII.

At the ramshackle Musician's Club, Zamp noted several performers from his old troupe, who evidently had not secured employment with Garth Ashgale. Paying them no heed, he posted a placard on the announcement board:

> The new *Miraldra's Enchantment*, managed by Apollon Zamp, winner at the Lanteen Competition, has openings for several excellent and versatile musicians, who play instruments of the following categories:
>> Belp-horn, screedle, cadenciver, variboom, elf-pipe, tympany, guitar, dulciole, heptagong, zinfonella.
> Auditions will be granted aboard *Miraldra's*

Enchantment (formerly the *Universal Pancomium*) at Bynum's Dock.

The orchestra ultimately selected will participate in an important and innovative program, to be presented before King Waldemar at the Mornune Festival.

Only dedicated and expert artists will be considered. Remuneration will be in appropriate measure.

Even before Zamp had finished posting his notice, every musician present had come to lean over his shoulder and read the announcement, with the exception only of some of Zamp's former employees, who showed disinterest or diffidence.

Zamp responded to the questions with brief remarks: "Employment is of long or indefinite duration." "I can use no bagpipes nor water-organs." "Living conditions are to be more than adequate." "Yes, we definitely play at Mornune and I hope to win the grand prize." "The treasure will be shared in some degree." "Security? Safety? The ship will be equipped with effective and modern protective devices. I foresee no problems." "Auditions will start today at the third gong of the afternoon."

Zamp returned to his punt and was taken to the Entertainers, Mimes and Magicians' Social Club where he posted a second notice and responded to a similar set of questions. As he departed the premises, he met Viliweg the prestidigitator face to face.

Viliweg, wearing a suit of black gabardine, a cape of mouse-colored taupe, a rakish, long-billed cap and various items of jewelry, seemed nothing less than prosperous. At the sight of Zamp, he nodded curtly and would have proceeded past, but Zamp held up his hand. "A moment, Viliweg! I would like a few words with you."

"I am somewhat pressed for time," said Viliweg. "Unfortunately I cannot indulge myself in the pleasure of conversation."

"The matter is of considerable importance," said Zamp. "Would you care to step to the side of the veranda?"

Viliweg stamped his foot in annoyance. "I recall no matters of outstanding urgency."

Zamp said gently, "I will refresh your memory." He took Viliweg's elbow and led him to a secluded area behind a screen of decorative ferns. "Apparently," said Zamp, "you failed to secure a post with Garth Ashgale?"

"Bah," grumbled Viliweg. "Ashgale, like many other ship-masters, is highly verbal but significantly less adept when it comes to action."

"Still," Zamp remarked, "you appear quite prosperous. This is surely a new suit, and new boots as well."

Viliweg blew out his cheeks. "I have ample resources."

"The valuable ornament you are wearing on your cap," said Zamp, "may I examine it?"

"I do not care to disarrange my dress," said Viliweg. "Now, if you will excuse me—"

"Not so fast," said Zamp with a meaningful leer. "I am also interested in that clasp of topaz and silver which pins your cloak. Their familiarity haunts me, and not to make too large a matter of it, be so good as to return my property before I slash away your ears with two strokes of my sabre."

Viliweg made the usual expostulations, but in the end Zamp recovered a number of his jewels, together with a pouch containing a hundred and twelve iron groats.

"Now to the other phase of my business with you," said Zamp. "I am re-forming the troupe, and I direct your attention to the placard I have just now posted. I possibly may be able to write into *Macbeth* the part of an expert prestidigitator; if you are interested, please report to Bynum's Dock tomorrow morning.''

"I have just lost the savings of a lifetime," said Viliweg in a morose voice. "Now I must return to work. Ah, well, at the very least I find a loyal employer who rises to the occasion when hardship threatens.'' He tried to embrace Zamp, but Zamp stepped alertly back and after verifying his pouch for the jewels, departed the premises.

In yet another quarter of Coble Zamp posted a placard announcing possible employment for a number of personable girls of good voice and nimble body; then in good spirits he returned to Bynum's Dock. Perhaps the loss of his wonderful ship was not unalloyed tragedy after all. New challenges confronted him; if surmounted they would yield rewards greater than any he had ever previously considered. Life was too short for either pessimism or complacency!

At Bynum's Dock he paused in surprise. Where were the carpenters, painters, riggers and victualers, who at this moment should have been plying their various trades? He marched aboard the ship, ignoring Berard's demand for an admission fee, and discovered Gassoon at his display of ancient garments with a party of sightseers. "—nothing more fascinating than style," Gassoon intoned. "Of all the symbols by which men and women reveal themselves, none are more subtle, yet explicit, than the garments which they choose to represent their guises. Garments have a vitality—yes, Zamp?'' This in response to Zamp's signal.

"I would like a word or two with you."

"Be so good as to await me in my office."

Zamp, however, stalked out upon the foredeck. Twenty minutes later, Gassoon peered out the door, and, spying Zamp, joined him.

"I understood that you were to await me in my office," Gassoon complained. "I have been to inconvenience looking about the ship!"

Zamp controlled his temper. "Where are the workmen? I expected activity; I find torpor."

"For the best of reasons," said Gassoon. "The project is beyond my capacity. I cannot afford to spend so much iron."

Zamp gritted his teeth. "What of our plans; what of the great adventures we had promised ourselves?"

"In due course, and on a less extravagant scale. The Damsel Blanche-Aster and I will give readings to audiences along the Vissel; there is no need for vast exploits."

"Aha!" said Zamp, "Damsel Blanche-Aster has concurred in these plans?"

"I have no doubt as to her acquiescence. She is a rare soul and shares my love for the rich, the real, the authentic."

"We shall soon find out," said Zamp, "because she is coming aboard at this minute."

Gassoon strode off to greet Damsel Blanche-Aster, with Zamp coming behind.

Like Zamp, Damsel Blanche-Aster seemed puzzled in regard to the inactivity aboard the ship. Gassoon anticipated her question. "My dear young lady, it is always a pleasure to see you! I have formulated a variation of our plans which I know will please you. The way to Mornune is long; an extravagant production such as that Zamp proposes will cost a large sum, and in the last analysis we are interested in resurrecting classic art, not vainglory—"

Damsel Blanche-Aster asked in a cool voice, "You are bored with our glorious scheme?"

"Bored? Never! Still, I must reckon expense; the

costs are exorbitant; I now envision a more modest program—"

Damsel Blanche-Aster handed him a pouch of embroidered green silk. "Here is two pounds of iron. Is that sufficient? It is all I have."

Gassoon stammered and passed the pouch from hand to hand as if it were hot. "Of course; these are ample funds, but I conceived—"

"We have no time for indecision," said Damsel Blanche-Aster. "The Mornune Festival is almost upon us, and we can't delay. You are sure the iron will cover expenses?"

"In grand style," said Zamp. "What with the iron Master Gassoon himself is prepared to spend, we can now mount a production not only to entertain King Waldemar, but to dazzle him!"

Throdorus Gassoon threw up his hands. "If this is the way it must be— " he drew a deep breath, "—well, then, I am the man for it! Berard! Summon the shipwrights! No more visitors to the museum! There is work to be done!"

Chapter 10

Two weeks wrought significant changes upon the old *Universal Pancomium*. Gassoon had grudgingly yielded the forward area of his museum to a stage and the foredeck had been altered to allow the placement of benches. Blue, yellow and red trim enlivened the white and black; the masts had been scraped and varnished; gonfalons, banderoles, bunting and angel-traps had been lavishly affixed to stays and shrouds. All in all, the gaunt old vessel made a brave show at its Bynum's Dock moorings.

Zamp had assembled a troupe which he considered adequate to his purposes, though Gassoon had made stentorian objections when six shapely mime-girls joined the company. "Where will we require six such females in our production? There is no mention whatever of such persons!"

"The 'Dramatis Personae' requires attendants," replied Zamp. "Need they be old and lank and toothless?"

"Need they be pivoting red-haired maenads?" countered Gassoon.

"Such creatures decorate a production," explained Zamp. "Additionally, I plan to make the most of those references to banquets and celebrations, naturally with due faithfulness to the text. These girls will augment the verisimilitude of such scenes.''

Gassoon had more to say but in the end walked away waving his hands in the air.

Damsel Blanche-Aster worked diligently at the part of-Lady Macbeth, while Zamp himself performed Macbeth. Gassoon had agreed to act the part of Duncan, while Viliweg was cast as Banquo, and Zamp had in mind several innovations to take advantage of Viliweg's special talents.

During rehearsals camp attempted to simplify and modernize certain obscure phrases, and again found himself in controversy with Gassoon, who insisted on fidelity to the original. "All very well," cried Zamp, "but speech is spoken that it may be understood. Why present a drama which simply bewilders everyone?"

"Your mind lacks poetry," Gassoon responded sharply. "Can you not imagine a drama of hints and dreams which totally transcends the animal titillations and spasms and hooting sounds upon which your reputation is based?"

"These qualities won me the invitation to play before King Waldemar," retorted Zamp. "Hence they must be accorded respect."

"Very well! Play your vapidities before King Waldemar if you like, but for the rest, I refuse to compromise!"

The musical score to *Macbeth* posed a different set of problems. Gassoon contended that the drama could well be played without music; Zamp, however, cited references to music and song, as well as fanfares, flourishes of hautboys, gongs and the like, which Gassoon could not dispute.

"Authenticity must be our watchword," said Gassoon. "Since the text specifies the music of hautboys, clari-

ons and gongs, these instruments would seem to consti-
tute the accompanying orchestra.''

Zamp refused to consider such a limitation, which
perhaps prompted Gassoon to obduracy when it came to
fixing upon a date of departure from Coble. ''Our
business is at Mornune,'' argued Zamp. ''Far better to
arrive three days early with a makeshift curtain-drop
than three days late with all working to perfection!''

''Let us avoid frantic haste,'' returned Gassoon. ''I
am not a man to run naked out into the street at the
smell of smoke. Here is the place to perfect our equipment and to verify the quality of our company. I do not
intend to risk either my life, or my ship, or the artistic
nature of my productions merely to soothe your nervousness.''

''Must I point out over and over that our association
is based upon winning the competition at Mornune?''

''I wish you well,'' said Gassoon in his driest voice,
''so long as my own aspirations are not thwarted in the
process.''

Gassoon at last agreed to sail immediately after the
annual fair at Coble, which opened two days hence.
''We can present our opening performances to the
throng,'' said Gassoon, ''and the receipts will defray
some of the terrible expense to which I have been put.''

The lure of profits to be earned at the fair attracted
others to Coble. On the evening of the same day
Fironzelle's Golden Conceit sailed into port, red and
purple bunting fluttering from every stay, lamps flash-
ing at the mastheads, musicians playing a rousing tune
on the foredeck. The ship tied up at Zulman's Dock, a
hundred yards north of *Miraldra's Enchantment*, and a
few minutes later Garth Ashgale appeared on his ceremonial visit. He stepped on board wearing an expression of wonder. ''Throdorus Gassoon—this is you indeed,

but is this the staid old *Universal Pancomium?* By my life, you have bedizened yourself!''

Gassoon gestured toward Zamp, coming down the ladder from the quarterdeck. ''You must credit my associate for the transformation.''

Garth Ashgale laughed incredulously. ''Apollon Zamp! I heard that you had taken employment aboard the *Two Varminies* as an exotic dancer!''

''This is the second *Miraldra's Enchantment*,'' said Zamp evenly. ''When I return from Mornune I plan to construct the most marvelous boat of the ages: *The Third Enchantment*.''

Garth Ashgale showed an expression of concern and surprise. ''Do you still intend the rigors of the Upper Vissel and Bottomless Lake?''

''Rigors?'' demanded Gassoon sharply. ''What rigors?''

''Reefs, shoals and rapids can be overcome by exact seamanship. Far worse are the river pirates and the Akgal slave-takers who infest this area. Garken, as you know, is their depot.''

''We are equipped with the most modern equipment,'' sid Zamp. ''We fear the Akgals no more than waterdogs.''

''You are more confident than I,'' said Ashgale. ''I admire such daring! As for me I intend a placid cruise up the Suanol.'' He looked around the ship. ''You have made a hundred changes. What will be your performance? More of the old routines?''

''Definitely not,'' declared Gassoon. ''We are playing a program of ancient Earthly classics: works which have survived the centuries!''

''Most interesting! When will be your first performance?''

''In two days.''

''I will be sure to attend at least one performance,'' said Ashgale. ''Who knows? I might learn something!''

Ashgale departed. Gassoon said pettishly: "You insisted that the Upper Vissel was utterly safe! Now Ashgale tells bloodcurdling tales of slave-takers!"

"Let him talk as he will!" scoffed Zamp. "His motives are not at all obscure."

Zamp attended the evening performance aboard *Fironzelle's Golden Conceit*, and was forced to admit that the production went in a manner as smooth, suave and elegant as Garth Ashgale himself.

After the performance, Zamp strolled along the dock to the Downstream Tavern, where showboat personnel tended to gather. He took a jug of beer to a booth at the side of the room, and seated himself in the shadows.

Performers began to arrive, alone or in groups of two or three. Zamp noticed several of his former employees, among them Wilver the Water-walker, who performed his miraculous feats with the aid of glass stilts. He was joined by Gandolf and Thymas, the two most striking grotesques of Zamp's former troupe. Wilver, Gandolf and Thymas seated themselves in the booth next to that where Zamp sat, and called to the attendant for beer. For a moment Zamp heard only the clink of jug and mug, which by some tick of acoustics reached his ears with great clarity, and then conversation:

"Long and prosperous life to us all!" This was the voice of Wilver.

Another brief pause; then Gandolf said in a melancholy voice, "I fear that we have selected the wrong profession."

Thymas said, "The difficulty lies not with the profession, but with the vultures who control our livelihoods."

"True! It was hard to settle upon the worst, although several names come to mind. Apollon Zamp is as full-fledged a rascal as any."

"Why slight Garth Ashgale, who straightens his garments and adjusts his hair before he dares look at himself in a mirror?"

"For sheer double-dealing, I prefer Zamp. For tricks he outclasses a two-headed hoop-snake on ice."

Wilver said, "In my opinion, Ashgale is both more clever and more guileful. Zamp is simply crude and offensive."

"Ah, well," sighed Gandolf, "the topic is sterile. Do you intend to continue with Ashgale? He plans a tour up the Suanol, so far as Blackwillow."

"No, I find the air of that particular region too harsh to breathe, and in any event Ashgale has ended my employment."

"And mine as well."

"So! That villain Ashgale has discharged us all!"

Zamp again heard the thud of jugs being placed down upon the table. Then Wilver spoke, "So, now, we must begin anew, or rot here in Coble."

Gandolf gave a morose grunt. "That devil's arse-wipe Zamp is forming a new troupe. No doubt he would rejoice to see us all."

"He'll never see me!" declared Thymus. "Rather than serve that long-tongued scoundrel, I'll cut basket-withe."

"I also refuse to be despoiled," said Wilver. "Shall we drink more beer?"

"Gladly, except that I can spare no more iron."

"Nor I."

"In that case, we might as well be off."

Zamp watched the three cross the room and go out the door. He finished the beer remaining in the jug, then put his hands down upon the table in preparation for leaving, when into the tavern came Damsel Blanche-Aster escorted by Throdorus Gassoon. Zamp slumped back into the darkest corner of the booth and pulled the cap over his face. Gassoon, noticing the vacant booth, steered Damsel Blanche-Aster across the room and seated her with gallant punctilio.

"Well, then, my dear," said Gassoon, "I take pleasure in introducing you to the traditional resort of the showboat troupes. Look around you; you will notice members of Ashgale's company, as well as several folk from our own small enterprise. And with what might you care to refresh yourself?"

"Merely a cup of tea."

"Ah, but my dear! Surely a potion more warm, more pervasive, more—shall I say—intimate?"

"Just tea, please."

There was a brief silence; Damsel Blanche-Aster might have been looking about the room. "Why did you bring me here?"

"Because I wanted to talk to you. Aboard ship that hobgoblin Zamp seems to be everywhere, as if there were four of him. Wherever I look his face pops out."

"So then?"

"A moment; here is the waiter." Gassoon ordered tea and a small flask of wine, then turned his attention back to Damsel Blanche-Aster. "You are a principal in our production; how do you think it is going?"

"The effect is striking and unique, if nothing else."

"This may be—but is it art?"

"I don't know what 'art' is." Damsel Blanche-Aster's voice was so pensive that Zamp had difficulty hearing.

Gassoon became ponderously facetious. "What? A woman of your intelligence? I will never believe it!"

Zamp could almost see Damsel Blanche-Aster's disinterested shrug. She said, "I suspect that the word was invented by second-rate intelligences to describe the incomprehensible activities of their betters."

Gassoon chuckled. "The word defines a way of life. I am no artist; I wish I were! At the very least we can, in our small way, function as organs of dissemination." Gassoon made a clicking sound. "If only we could rid ourselves of Zamp!"

"Master Zamp provides us safe-conduct across the Bottomless Lake."

Gassoon's voice became fretful. "Why should we undertake that awful voyage? At Coble, along the Lower Vissel, the river runs calm; we can ignore the dangerous and paltry and sordid as if they were the essence of nothing!"

"First we must go to Mornune."

"But why?" Gassoon's voice was a petulant bleat. "I fail to understand!"

Damsel Blanche-Aster seemed to sigh. "You will never rest until you learn my motives."

"Exactly so!" Gassoon now became arch. "Shall I tell you why?"

Damsel Blanche-Aster made no audible response.

Gassoon said, "I dread the possibility of a far lover."

Damsel Blanche-Aster's voice was soft and even. "No such lover exists. My father was a nobleman of East Llorel. At Castle Araflame he owned a chest of precious books, which were stolen by my Uncle Tristan, and taken to his palace in Mornune. Both uncle and father are dead; my brother holds Araflame and the chest of rare books in Mornune is mine; I need merely claim them."

Zamp, sitting in the next booth, pursed his lips and nodded thoughtfully. Gassoon exclaimed in wonder. "You have seen these books?"

"Not for several years. When we arrive at Mornune, we shall examine them together."

"There will be no difficulty in claiming them?"

"None whatever."

Gassoon made a plaintive nasal sound. "Then perhaps we should attempt the journey after all."

"That has always been the plan."

The two sat in silence for a moment or two, then Gassoon heaved a sigh. "I distrust that fellow Zamp. For all his prancing bonhomie he is devious, and I dislike the lascivious manner in which he ogles you."

"He is perfectly inconsequential, except for the safe conduct he carries."

"In that case, let us talk of ourselves. The perfect union derives from a sharing of dreams. From this point of view we are a single soul, and now why should not we profess this unity with all the strength of our persons? Come, give me your hand; let me caress it!"

Damsel Blanche-Aster's response was light and easy. "Throdorus Gassoon, you are as impetuous as a mythical hero. I am shy. You must restrain your fervor until our acquaintance ripens."

Gassoon groaned. "How long then?"

"I will tell you when the time arrives; meanwhile you must not mention the matter."

"Your modesty does you credit. Still, should we suspend ourselves in a soulless ether while bubbles of bliss float past uncaptured? Our lives do not last forever!"

"In the abstract," said Damsel Blanche-Aster, "I share your feelings. Shall we leave? There is nothing here to interest me. I have already seen enough dancers and actors to serve me all my life."

Gassoon and Damsel Blanche-Aster departed the tavern. Anticipating no more entertainment, Zamp followed soon after.

In the morning Zamp conducted a dress rehearsal. In his role as Macbeth, he thought it necessary to demonstrate the emotional ties between Macbeth and Lady Macbeth (played with casual insouciance by Damsel Blanche-Aster). He embraced her ardently on several occasions, until at last Gassoon, as Duncan, called out a reprimand: "The text specifies no such passionate gropings! This is serious drama, not a lewd pantomime!"

"I must be the judge of what constitutes dramatic impact," said Zamp. "Your own delivery, for instance, is not altogether faultless, and if we are to win at Mornune we all must project an authentic emotion. Perhaps we should introduce a scene with Macbeth and his lady on their couch—"

"There is absolutely no need for such an exposition," stated Gassoon. "Let us proceed."

Zamp signaled the orchestra. "From the beginning of the scene."

Shortly before noon Zamp was notified that certain persons wished to speak with him. On the gangway stage waited Wilver the Water-walker, together with the grotesques Gandolf and Thymas.

"Good morning, gentlemen!" said Zamp. "Our last meeting, so I recall, was under less happy circumstances."

"Do you refer to the Lanteen sandbar or to the Green Star Inn?" asked Wilver. "I seem to recall some good-natured banter on both occasions, which helped mitigate the tragedy at Port Whant."

"Possibly true. It is indeed pleasant to see you, and I wish you well in your new careers with Garth Ashgale."

Gandolf spat over the gangplank into the river. "Ashgale lacks real competence. His productions never approach the quality we took for granted on the old *Miraldra's Enchantment*."

Wilver the Water-walker remarked, "Ah, the old troupe! Those were halcyon days!"

Thymas said, "Ashgale supplied us transportation

back to Coble, true enough, but now I too am considering a change.''

Wilver the Water-walker said thoughtfully, "I would resign my important position in an instant to rejoin the old troupe! What do you say, Master Zamp? Why should we not revive the glorious old times?''

"Never be guided by sentimentality!" advised Zamp. "I advise you all to remain with Garth Ashgale, whose terms of employment are stable; as I recall, he discharges only the notoriously incompetent.''

"He can also be a difficult taskmaster," grumbled Wilver. "He wants me to perform my act without glass stilts, which is difficult.''

"We all have similar problems with Ashgale," said Thymas. "For instance, in his production *The Extraordinary Dream of Countess Ursula*, Gandolf and I must simulate strange animals in questionable poses.''

"I believe, all taken with all, that I will accept Master Zamp's offer," said Gandolf.

"I likewise.''

"And I.''

Zamp shrugged. "As you wish. I have no present need for a water-walker; Wilver must serve as an apprentice grotesque. You must all supplement your duties as grooms to the bullocks. Your stipends will not be large, since Master Gassoon is a practical man. You may bring your effects aboard at once.''

Wilver, Gandolf and Thymas slowly descended the gangplank, muttering to each other.

To the annual fair came folk from along the shores of Surmise Bay, from everywhere about the Delta, from as far up-river as Badburg, from places even more remote: Iona on the Suanol, Byssus on the Wergence, Funk's Grove on the Lant, the travelers arriving by way of Nestor on the Murne. The inns of Coble were suddenly crowded with a diversity of people, and Waterfront Avenue seethed and pulsed with their costumes. Along the docks temporary booths displayed artifacts, oils, essences and balsams; also, sausages from Verlory on the Murne, potted reed-bird from Port Optimo, candied ginger and pickled mace from Callou across Surmise Bay. The glassblowers of Lanteen offered utensils, carboys, flasks, cups and dishes, as well as toys and little glass animals. The Ratwick tanneries displayed hides along a row of redolent racks; agents of the Wigtown looms draped their cloth over lines strung between lime trees; the Coble factors sold shoes, sandals, boots, hats, cloaks, breeches, jackets and shirts to the outlanders.

During the morning Garth Ashgale advertised his performance with pyrotechnics, balloons, and a parade up and down the waterfront, and his afternoon performance was played to an overflow audience. Throdorus Gassoon scorned what he called "flummox and puffery." "We are not interested in sensation-seekers," he told Zamp. "Let them waste their iron!" Nonetheless, a large number of folk turned away from *Fironzelle's Golden Conceit* and paid their way aboard *Miraldra's Enchantment*. Gassoon was pleased to hear the clink of iron.

Zamp thought that the performance went off tolerably well, although Damsel Blanche-Aster still brought to the part of Lady Macbeth a debonair facility which distressed Gassoon. The audience seemed not to heed this particular shortcoming, if such it were. They sat entranced, or perhaps bemused, apparently convinced that a production so obscure must necessarily be significant, and at the finale applauded politely, though without hysterical enthusiasm. Gassoon, on the whole, felt encouraged by the day's work, although the incidental business and specialties which Zamp had introduced received what he considered unwarranted approval.

On the morning after the close of the fair, *Miraldra's Enchantment* sailed north from Coble. At the last minute Gassoon became nervous and declared the vessel not yet ready for so far a journey. Zamp, choking on his impatience, insisted that the boat would never be more ready. "The monsoon blows up-river; time presses hard on us! Let us be off!"

Gassoon made a flapping desperate gesture, which the deckhands interpreted as a signal to cast off lines. Bullocks heaved at the capstans; the stern-paddle groaned and creaked; the great boat eased away from Bynum's Dock and out into the stream. The sails billowed, rippled loosely and were sheeted home; *Miraldra's Enchantment* moved north.

Chapter 11

For three days *Miraldra's Enchantment* enjoyed a wind so fair that even Gassoon showed no inclination to halt; the towns Spanglemar, Wigtown and Port Moses were passed and left astern.

Garth Ashgale, bound for the settlements of the High Suanol under the Lornamay Hills, had departed Coble a day previously to *Miraldra's Enchantment*. At Ratwick *Fironzelle's Golden Conceit* was discovered moored to the single dock. Zamp and Gassoon agreed that no good purpose could be served by anchoring in the stream to await Ashgale's departure, and *Miraldra's Enchantment* continued up-river.

Late in the afternoon, with the wind faltering, Gassoon decided to sail behind that tract of land known as Harbinger Island, in order to play a program at Chist, a village usually avoided by reason of its poverty and somewhat inconvenient location. The *River Index* described Chist as:

a generally placid village of five hundred population, originally settled by a band of Fundamental Vitalists fleeing the persecutions of the Grand Doctrinate at Chiasm, Lune XXIII Central. The Chists are ruled by a matriarchy and observe a number of peculiar taboos, none of which need overly concern the cautious ship-master. So long as he makes no reference to local conditions, he will find the folk of Chist a disciplined and attentive audience. No great profit can be expected, as payments are ordinarily made in barter.

Gassoon ignored Zamp's unenthusiastic report, and took the showboat up to the rickety pier. As soon as the gangplank was extended, a pair of song-girls carried placards down to the dock. One depicted a mailed warrior hacking apart his adversary, and bore the legend:

MACBETH
An Epic of Ancient Earth

On the other a woman with flying yellow hair held aloft a bloody dagger. The inscription read:

MACBETH
The Murderous Rites of Ancient Earth

Gassoon stepped out upon the gangway stage to address the crowd of villagers. For the occasion he had donned a black cape and a tall-crowned, narrow-brimmed black hat, under which tufts of white hair thrust forth to right and left. He held up his arms in a commanding gesture. "Dignitaries and gentlefolk of Chist! I am Throdorus Gassoon and I am privileged to come before you with my wonderful vessel and my band of artists and musicians. Prepare yourself for an emotional experience the like of which you have never known! We are prepared to present before you an authentic drama of ancient Earth!"

An old woman called up: "Does that mean real killing?"

"My dear lady, of course not!"

The old woman spat toward the posters. "So much for your advertising."

Gassoon in some perplexity came down off the gang-plank and examined the placards which he had not before seen. Zamp was forced to concede that Gassoon encompassed the situation with aplomb. "These plac-ards," stated Gassoon, "represent the theme of *Macbeth* in bold symbols; like all symbols they must not be mistaken for the products they advertise."

Another old woman said briskly, "Well, then, to negotiate for the entire village—what will be your fee, symbols and all?"

"Our prices are very fair," said Gassoon. "For the entire village I must reckon on a crowd of total capacity."

Eventually Gassoon agreed to accept, in lieu of iron, a ton of cattle fodder, six measures of bog syrup and a quantity of smoked eel.

At dusk the lamps were lit and immediately the popu-lation of the village began to board the vessel. men, women and children; and in short order the benches were crowded, although the stipulated commodities had not yet been delivered. Gassoon protested to the chief matriarch who threw back her head in annoyance. "We never pay until we test the goods. If your performance is largely symbolic, as I understood you to say, then our fee will also be symbolic."

"This is unacceptable," stormed Gassoon. "Deliver the fodder, the syrup and the eel, or we will perform no masterpiece whatever!"

The matriarch declared that she would not be so hoodwinked, but a man who had gone aboard the *Two Varminies* at Badburg assured her that Gassoon's conditions were not unusual, and finally the produce was delivered to the ship. Gassoon gave a signal; the tympanist sounded gongs and the orchestra played that rousing tune which Zamp had contrived as an overture.

The curtain drew back to display a dismal wasteland. Rocks jutted into a black sky; the set was illuminated by a pair of flaming torches. Three witches crouched about a fire where a caldron seethed. Rather than immediately entering the dialogue, which Zamp considered abrupt, the witches cavorted in an odd triangular dance, toward and away from the fire, employing gestures at once wild yet controlled, to suggest a weight of purposeful evil. Finally, drained of their frenzy, the witches lurched to the fire, to sag into misshapen wads of black and brown rags.

The music halted; dead silence smothered the stage. In a sour-sweet voice the first witch spoke:

> When shall we three meet again,
> In thunder, lightning or in rain?

Zamp, at the drawing of the curtains, had noticed a stir of tension in the audience. The witches danced to furtive snickers from the men and hisses of indrawn breath from the women.

> Fair is foul and foul is fair;
> Hover through the fog—

One of the matriarchs stepped forward, and spreading wide her arms stopped the performance. "We did not pay produce to suffer your mockeries!"

Gassoon ran forth in a fury. "What is this? Please seat yourself, madame; you are disturbing our performance!"

"This is our performance! We paid for it!"

"Well, yes, this is true enough—"

"So, then, we want it altered. These caricatures offend us all!"

"Impossible!" cried Gassoon in a brassy voice. "We follow the authentic text. Be so good as to resume your seat. The drama will proceed."

The matriarch sullenly returned to her seat; the scene changed and Gassoon came onto the stage as Duncan:

> What bloody man is that? He can report
> As seemeth by his plight, of the revolt
> The newest state.

Watching from the wings Zamp noticed that the audience seemed uncommonly attentive. Their eyes glinted with torchlight reflections and they sat stiffly erect.

Scene 3: the witches once more occupied the stage. Certain young men in the audience could not suppress their amusement. The matriarch rose to her feet and pounded with her staff. "I have seen enough. Remove our goods; it is precisely as I had feared."

Gassoon sprang forward. "Be calm, all! Resume your seats! We will play the drama without the witches!"

Zamp, with somewhat more experience, gave other orders: "Slip the hawsers! Pressure on the pumps! Tilt the deck!"

The ship floated away from the dock; the enraged folk of Chist were washed down the decks into the water. The stern-wheel churned and the vessel swept off upstream, around Harbinger Island and back to the main channel of the Vissel River. The evening was dead calm; the vessel anchored in midstream, and the remainder of the night passed placidly.

* * *

On the next afternoon Gassoon guided *Miraldra's Enchantment* to Port Optimo, and ordained another performance of *Macbeth*. Zamp consulted the *River Index* and once again approached Gassoon with his findings. "The situation is less clear here than at Chist, but I find compelling reasons for a change or two. For instance: the folk here abominate the use of alcohol. Hence, Macbeth poisons Duncan by serving him a goblet of brandy. Additionally, rather than witches, we had best use water-wefkins."

Gassoon could hardly find words. "The integrity of our work will be compromised!"

"The *River Index* points out that Port Optimo maintains three longboats equipped with fire-harpoons. It will not be feasible to wash tonight's audience off the deck."

Gassoon threw his long arms into the air, as if gripping an imaginary overhead bar. "Make only those changes which are absolutely necessary."

Either because of, or in spite of, Zamp's improvisations, the evening's performance was received with approbation. Gassoon still was not pleased. He took exception to the Act Three banquet, during which Macbeth, as king, commanded jugglers, dancers and acrobats to provide entertainment for the court, which entertainment continued for the better part of an hour. Gassoon also criticized the episodes of marital tenderness which Zamp had seen fit to insert into the drama.

On the following day, with sails taut before a fair wind, *Miraldra's Enchantment* drove north past Badburg and on to Fwyl, where the *Pamellissa* and the *Melodious Hour* were already moored; and Gassoon refused to present a program under the circumstances.

After Fwyl the winds became capricious. During the afternoon of the third day *Miraldra's Enchantment* swept grandly around Glassblower's Point, across the swirl of the Lant current and up to the Lanteen dock, where Zamp and Gassoon had agreed on a two or three day layover.

The following morning Gassoon opened his museum to the Lanteen public, and Zamp took advantage of his preoccupation to suggest an outing to Damsel Blanche-Aster. She at first gave a curt refusal; then, faced with the prospect of a day of boredom, she asked what he had in mind.

Zamp had not yet formed definite plans; on the spur of the moment he proposed a visit to the glassworks. "The artisans are most clever and skillful; to watch them at work is said to be fascinating."

"Very well then. Is it far?"

"Just around the hill. Let's leave at once before Gassoon thinks of something for us to do."

Damsel Blanche Aster laughed with such freedom and gaiety that Zamp wondered how he could have ever thought her constrained. She seemed to fall in with Zamp's mood; like truant children they slipped from the boat and walked up the esplanade.

Damsel Blanche-Aster now decided that rather than a visit to the glassworks, she preferred to climb to the top of the hill. Zamp readily agreed, and they turned into a lane which angled up Glassblower's Bluff, back and forth between hedges and low stone walls.

Today, through quirk, or caprice, or mood or optimism, Damsel Blanche-Aster put no constraints on her conduct. Zamp had never seen her so animated. Her pale hair blew in the wind; her eyes shone the clear gray-blue of a mountain lake; in her white frock she might have been a simple girl of the countryside, and Zamp thought her completely charming. Pausing to admire a quaint little cottage built of bulbous green glass flasks, she remarked at the flowers and even chirruped at the child playing with toy glass animals on the stoop.

They proceeded up the lane, which became a track winding up the slope past pens and pastures, then steeply up the final crag toward the sky, where puffs of clouds drifted north. Abandoning all dignity, Damsel Blanche-Aster ran up the trail, pausing to pick wildflowers or toss pebbles down-slope, while Zamp marched behind, longing to participate in the frolic, yet hardly daring to intrude without an invitation. They gained the summit and stood in sun and wind, with cloud-shadows racing across the landscape far below. Lanteen straggled along the Lant from River House on the east jetty to the Green Star Inn on its crooked stilts to the west.

Damsel Blanche-Aster climbed upon a rock and scanned the circle of the horizon, dwelling longest on the way to the north, along the mighty Vissel. She bent to descend from the rock. Zamp was on hand, and nothing could be easier as she jumped down than to catch her in his arms. For an instant it seemed that she became supple; then immediately she stiffened and slid away. Zamp was not pleased; it was almost as if absent-mindedly she had thought herself on the hill with some dream-person, only to discover, almost instantly, that the person was Apollon Zamp.

Damsel Blanche-Aster sat down in the shelter of the rock, away from the wind. Zamp joined her, and intoxicated with her proximity, slid his arm around her waist.

Damsel Blanche-Aster turned him a glance of frosty inquiry and rose to her feet; Zamp clasped her legs and looked up imploringly. "Why are you so cruelly cold? Do you love someone else?"

"I love no one."

"Do you swear it? Tell me the truth!"

"Master Zamp, please control yourself; you are becoming emotional."

"Emotional? I am in a frenzy! My brain feels like the Hall of Mirrors aboard the *Fire-glass Prism*; from every direction your face looks at me. I ache, I suffer, I am sick with longing! I think only of your wonderful beauty!"

Damsel Blanche-Aster laughed. "Master Zamp, you really become absurd."

"You are the absurd one! How can you be so cold? Compared to you, a statue of Saint Imola carved from ice is a madcap."

Damsel Blanche-Aster detached herself from Zamp's embrace. "Your doctrines are remarkable! As if I existed only to fulfill your cravings! Then, since I do not care to do so, the cosmos must be considered insane."

"It is more than craving," cried Zamp. "It is enchantment and wonder and dread—"

In spite of her professed indifference, Damsel Blanche-Aster was surprised. "Dread?"

"Dread for that time, which must arrive, if a hundred years from now, when I shall see you for the last time. I am content only in your presence; I adore you! In fact, yes! I will espouse you formally."

"I fear, Master Zamp, that you are a victim to your own perfervid imagination."

"Absolutely not! We sail to Mornune; promise that you will return with me!"

Damsel Blanche-Aster shook her head. "I have my own hopes and dreams."

Zamp shook his head in disbelief. "What must you do at Mornune, that you ignore the ardor of Apollon Zamp?"

"It is quite simple. I left Mornune to avoid espousal to a man I detest; now he is dead and I may return home."

"Astonishing!" declared Zamp. "Gassoon thinks you go to seek a treasure in rare books; you told me that you must save your sick father from imprisonment; now you remember this unwelcome suitor."

Damsel Blanche-Aster looked away to the north, and smiled a strange smile. "I am absentminded; I forget to whom I have made explanations."

Zamp hissed between his teeth. "You have tantalized me beyond endurance! Here and now we shall set matters to right!" Zamp stepped forward and took Damsel Blanche-Aster in his arms, only to receive a terrible blow on the head that brought tears to his eyes. For a period the sky rocked. A nasal voice rang in his ears: "Traitor and dog's vomit, I heard all I want to hear! Do you think you could deceive me with your skulking? Never! Prepare to die on this spot!"

Zamp, his eyes yet unfocused, glimpsed Gassoon brandishing a heavy cutlass. Frantically Zamp rolled aside and Gassoon's lunge went wide.

Zamp tried to scramble to his feet, to slip and fall sprawling again, while dodging Gassoon's second blow. Damsel Blanche-Aster ran forward and seized Gassoon's arm. "Throdorus! Calm yourself! Put up your blade!"

"I must destroy this vermin!" cried Gassoon. "He has performed a wicked act this morning!"

"He is foolish rather than evil. And remember! Only Zamp can provide us safe conduct across the Bottomless Lake!"

"This might be a sterile capability," Gassoon grumbled. He gave his cutlass a final flourish and addressed Zamp. "Consider yourself a dead man restored to life! I hope that you will be induced to mend your ways!"

Beside himself with fury, Zamp gained his feet and snatched forth his own blade. "Come now, you lank misfortune of a dog's miscarriage! Let us see whose life hangs by which thread! How dare you come spying on your betters?'' He stepped forward but Gassoon struck down with his cutlass and broke the shaft of Zamp's rapier and Zamp stood holding only the pommel.

Damsel Blanche-Aster took Gassoon's arm. "Come, Throdorus, let us ignore Master Zamp; he has lost his temper and is no longer coherent.'' She led Gassoon down the trail. Zamp sat down on a rock and massaged the side of his head. The episode seemed an incredible dream. How could any woman, alive and healthy, resist such importunities as those he had lavished upon Damsel Blanche-Aster? No matter! The voyage was not yet at its end. Zamp recalled that fractional instant when Damsel Blanche-Aster had seemed to melt. It was a positive sign, and Zamp would redouble his efforts. He would woo this exquisite creature with such gallantry as the world had never known! He would warm her icy heart with graceful occasions! He would quicken her pulse with music, fire her brain with poetry! She would learn to find him indispensable, and come to him brimming with love, beseeching his attention.

Zamp rose to his feet and found his hat He clapped it upon his head, and set off down the hill.

Returning to *Miraldra's Enchantment*, Zamp stalked up the gangplank with dignity. Gassoon greeted him coldly though without open rancor. The evening's performance went smoothly and Gassoon even seemed to approve certain of Zamp's embellishments which heretofore he had labeled "not authentic, opposite to the spirit of the original.''

On the following morning Zamp noticed that, contrary to his instructions, certain essentials were not being brought aboard the ship. He went at once to Gassoon's office, but found it empty; Gassoon was in the museum, displaying his collection of antique costumes to a group of local matrons. Gassoon pointedly ignored Zamp's signals and Zamp was forced to wait while Gassoon lovingly brought forth the old garments: imperial gowns, embroidered aprons, the black cassock of a Royal Skannic Lancer, the silks of a Lalustrine nymph, the costume of an ancient spaceman, and Gassoon's own favorite: a regal jacket brittle with age, embroidered lavishly in thread of green and tarnished gold. Gassoon discoursed upon each item in a reedy, droning voice until Zamp finally grew impatient. Grinning to himself he went to Gassoon's private office, entered and closed the door.

Within half a minute he heard hurried footsteps and Gassoon appeared. "What are you doing in here? This is my private office, where I do not welcome intruders."

"My apologies, Master Gassoon, but I wish to consult you on a matter of some urgency."

"Well then, what do you wish to discuss?"

It appears that I am not forceful enough with our shore agents. Yesterday I ordered aboard four bullocks to supplement our present eight beasts, together with ten tons of fodder. Nothing has yet been delivered and I would like you to take a hand in the matter."

"I canceled the order," snapped Gassoon, "which explains the whole situation."

"I did not order these bullocks out of idle caprice or in a spirit of self-indulgence," said Zamp. "The monsoon is starting to fail, and the journey is long; we should not put our faith in variable winds."

Gassoon made an incisive gesture with his big white hand. "The expense is beyond our prudent capacity; the issue is as simple as that. Even more to the point: I have developed very serious doubts about the whole wild scheme. Suppose we arrive at Mornune and fail in the competition? We have wasted a large sum of money for nothing.''

''We will not fail.''

Gassoon gave his head a mulish shake. ''The project is too risky, especially in view of the failing winds.''

''If we leave now there is no lack of time, even allowing for flawed winds.''

Again Gassoon shook his head. ''Frankly, I am discouraged. My hopes of producing classic drama have been eroded; at each performance you introduce some new innovation, and I am no longer surprised by anything, merely saddened. What is the point of proceeding?'' Gassoon paced back and forth across the office, with hands clasped behind his back. ''I fear that I have lost my illusions. In fact, you may now leave this vessel.''

''Indeed. And what of Damsel Blanche-Aster?''

''Her circumstances need not concern you in the slightest. She must be as bored as I am with harebrained exploits and impossible voyages. We will remain here at Lanteen for a week or two, then return by easy steps to Coble. Now, be so good as to leave this ship, or I will have Turliman put you ashore.''

''Just a moment.'' Leaving the office, Zamp stepped across the passageway to Damsel Blanche-Aster's cabin and knocked at the door. She looked forth.

''Come at once to Master Gassoon's office,'' said Zamp. ''He has an interesting announcement to make.''

Damsel Blanche-Aster, once more cool and intense, accompanied Zamp to Gassoon's office. Zamp made an airy salute in Gassoon's direction. ''Let us discuss your plans again, now that all those concerned are present.''

''There is nothing to discuss,'' stated Gassoon, in a voice like the middle tones of an oboe. ''I have determined that the voyage to Mornune is not only impractical and imprudent but dangerous. You, Zamp, are demonstrably an undesirable associate; you will leave the ship immediately. Daniel Blanche-Aster, we have many times celebrated our spiritual compatibility; the time perhaps has come to formalize our bond, to make us truly one.''

Damsel Blanche-Aster reflected a moment, then spoke in an uncharacteristically hesitant voice. ''Your judgments may well be correct, Throdorus. The journey north is toilsome, specially for a vessel such as this.''

Gassoon nodded grimly and darted a yellow glance toward Zamp.

Damsel Blanche-Aster spoke on in a musing voice. ''As you know, I have an affair at Mornune which must be settled before I can even comtemplate your other suggestions. Still, I believe that our various goals can be reconciled. You may return to me the two pounds of iron I advanced at Coble; Master Zamp will use this money to buy a felucca. He and I will sail north to Mornune as swiftly as may be. There I will accomplish my errand and Master Zamp may compete in the festival with my assistance—perhaps we will perform scenes from *Macbeth* or a program of comic pantomimes. Then, upon conclusion of the festival we will rejoin you here at Lanteen.''

The cords stood out along Gassoon's long neck; he opened his mouth to speak, but produced only a set of rasping sounds.

Zamp said thoughtfully, ''Such a plan seems feasible to me. In fact, it is our only alternative, since Master Gassoon does not care to venture north in his own vessel.'' He addressed himself to Damsel Blanche-Aster. ''I will go now and search out a suitable boat. Perhaps you could help Master Gassoon weigh out the two pounds of iron.''

Gassoon strode forward. "A moment, Master Zamp; not so fast, if you please. The situation is absurd. Do you think that I carry two pounds of iron in my pocket?"

"I don't know where you carry your iron, Master Gassoon. I only know that there is no time for delay. The monsoons are dying and we must reach Mornune."

Gassoon gave an angry croak of defeat. "Order aboard your four bullocks and your fodder. We sail for the north at once."

An hour before departure an item of unsettling news reached the ship, at which not even Zamp could rejoice, and which Gassoon greeted with a moan of despair. Near Bluskin on the Suanol a band of Dymnatic Black-Arrows had waylaid *Fironzelle's Golden Conceit*. They had captured Garth Ashgale with all his troupe and sunk the ship.

Chapter 12

Glassblower's Point dwindled to a blue-gray triangle low on the horizon and slowly merged into the haze, like a fading memory. Ahead, the Vissel extended between low banks, sometimes barely a quarter-mile wide, sometimes so broad that the total universe seemed to consist of water and sky. Consulting the *River Index*, Zamp discovered mention of only three settlements of consequence along the way to the Bottomless Lake: Skivaree, at the confluence of the Vissel and the Pelorus; Garken, a slave-traders' depot and caravan terminus; and Massacre Bend. Idanthus, Prairie View and Port Venable were places marked on the chart by hollow dots, to indicate a lack of definite information. Beyond Port Venable two hundred miles of wilderness were shown: swamp, steppe, an arm of the Tartark Forest; finally the Mandana Palisades and the Bottomless Lake.

The first day out of Lanteen the wind blew brisk, with tufts of cirrus scudding across the sky, and *Miraldra's Enchantment* drove up-river dragging a white moustache across the dun water.

On the following day the wind blew even more strongly. Long combings of stratus trailed across the sky, and at noon an ominous mass of nimbus came hulking up from the south. Gassoon nervously ordered in the foresail and mizzen, called for a reef in the mainsail, and the vessel lurched through a stormy afternoon, while Zamp put into rehearsal that version of *Macbeth* he would play at Mornune. Gassoon watched with a curled lip, then shaking his head in disgust, retired to his office. In addition to his witches' dance and banquet entertainments, Zamp now inserted sword-dancers, a coronation pageant, and an entire new sequence, to motivate the deceptions practiced upon Macbeth by the witches. At the opening of his new scene the three hags were discovered working over a great caldron, chanting spells, capering and clenching their hands, manipulating balls of blue fire, at last to produce (in the person of Deneis, the youngest of the mime-girls) a naked lank-haired lamia, who is then sent forth to suck the blood of Lady Macbeth in payment for the presages rendered Macbeth. Lady Macbeth awakens to find the lamia kneeling over her; the lamia flees and is then hunted down and killed in the forest, a scene which Zamp considered most effective. In revenge the witches instruct Macduff that his army must carry branches from Birnam Wood during their assault upon Dunsinane Castle. After the death of Macbeth and his lady, Zamp introduced an episode of somber pomp; the coronation of Malcolm, the new king, at Scone. Here Malcolm vows the extirpation of witchcraft, and the final scene is played once more on the darkling heath. The three witches at their fire cluck and chortle at King Malcolm's vain hopes, and address themselves to the invention of new intrigues and tragedies.

Mile after mile of the changeless river fell astern. At times a fisherman's hut stood on the bank, or a village of ten weatherbeaten cabins from which tousle-haired children tumbled forth to watch in wonder as the show-boat surged past.

On the fourth day out of Lanteen the river abruptly widened to become a placid flood, rippling and glinting in the sunlight, and presently the great Pelorus River could be discerned, making conflux from the northwest. The point of land between the two rivers displayed an irregular clutter of whitewashed houses: Skivaree.

According to the *River Index*, the folk of Skivaree were the survivors of a people from a land known as Kyl Wyff, far away to the east in Lune XXV. Omens discovered by their mantics had compelled them to migrate. A hundred years later thirty-four survivors had arrived at the Vissel where new omens commanded them to settle. By virtue of specialized skills they gained immunity from nomad attack and presently prospered; and now the Skivaree tattoo-masters, using fish-spine needles and secret inks, served all the tribes of the Tinsitala Steppe. At the Skivaree College of Decorum the daughters of nomad knights learned deportment, rug-weaving, saddle-making, the Dance of Four Move-ments and the Dance of Eight Movements. The *River Index* described the folk of Skivaree as affable, placid, tolerant. Despite all evidence to the contrary, they re-garded themselves as members of an extrahuman race, distinct from and superior to all other peoples of Big Planet. The *River Index* concluded with a rather chilling warning:

Guard your children with vigilance! Never allow them to wander the backstreets of Skivaree! With-out compunction the folk will seize them, wring their necks, butcher, dress, cook and serve them at table in any of a dozen modes, without guilt or afterthought. A full description of these odd folk is beyond the scope of this volume.

Gassoon decided to stop at Skivaree, both for the profit to be derived from a performance, and to purchase fresh greens and vegetables which had been in poor supply at Lanteen and to which he was partial. Zamp made no protest, and during the middle afternoon *Miraldra's Enchantment* warped alongside the Skivaree docks. Zamp set forth placards and proclaimed the evening's entertainment, while Gassoon went to inspect the market offerings.

With an hour or two of leisure on his hands Zamp strolled off in the company of Viliweg to investigate the town. The site of Skivaree, exposed to the river winds, had been blown bare; the stark whitewashed stone houses all faced south but showed no orderly placement, having been sited by omen. In a carefully delineated quarter along the Vissel were grouped the tattooing studios, three inns, five beer gardens, and a ground where visitors so inclined might set up their tents. Zamp saw men of a dozen varieties in as many distinctive costumes: Dymnatics, Varls seven feet tall, Gonchos with heads concealed under contrivances of leather and wood, Khouls with skins black as midnight, Lalukes wearing simulated tails, all drawn to Skivaree for the tattooing. As a rule they carried themselves with wary punctilio, each sort armed with their distinctive and special weapons, exchanging few words with one another, eyeing hereditary enemies askance, yet deterred from violence by the edicts of the tattoo-masters who wished no interference with their revenues. The folk of Skivaree, well-fleshed, round and bland of face, with sparse ginger-colored hair, resembled none of their patrons, and if they wished to think of themselves as a nonhuman race, Zamp was not prepared to dispute their conviction, so long as they paid their admission fees in sound black iron.

Returning to the boat, Zamp found that black iron

was the subject of discussion between Gassoon and an official of Skivaree, who declared that Gassoon's admission charges were unreasonable and exorbitant.

"Not so!" declared Gassoon. "Consider! I must invest in the boat and all my properties. Secondly, I must locate, hire, train, feed and pay an unreasonably large complement of actors, musicians and sailors. Thirdly, I journey a vast distance up this interminable river, earning no revenue until I arrive at Skivaree. Can you wonder that I am indignant when you tell me that my fees are too high?"

"There is something in what you say," agreed the official. "Still, at Skivaree we are seldom offered entertainment and everyone will wish to enjoy your presentation. But does any person wish to squander for two hours of passive pleasure the iron which he must labor an entire day to obtain?"

Gassoon gave his head an obstinate shake. "My fees are not too high. Your wage scale may simply be too low."

"Ah well, we shall see," said the official equably. "After all, what does it matter? Post your charges as high as you like; you will be assured a full audience in any case."

Shortly after sunset Gassoon opened the ticket window at the foot of the gangplank, while the orchestra on the quarterdeck played a series of rousing jigs and rounds. At once the folk of Skivaree appeared; and paying Gassoon's stipulated admission fee, filed aboard until every seat was occupied.

Zamp presented three introductory pieces: a pole-balancing act, Viliweg with his legerdemain, and a comic dance of clowns and simulated oels. Then the curtain rose on *Macbeth*.

Zamp was pleased with the effect of his innovations.

The audience sat in disciplined ranks, displaying fixed smiles of placid enjoyment. The final curtain elicited no overt approbation, and the audience filed quietly off the ship.

The civic official at once approached Gassoon. "A fine performance, excellent indeed, stinting nothing in zeal or duration. The musicians played to exact tempo; the substance of the drama was significant and timely."

Gassoon was immensely gratified. "It is generous of you to say as much, after our little discussion in regard to admission fees."

The official made a polite gesture. "What did it amount to? Nothing. While I am here we had best settle the matter of the dockage fee, which I computed during the performance." He handed Gassoon a slip of paper. "Here is the receipt; be so good as to pay me this weight of iron."

Gassoon reared back aghast. "Dockage fee? For a showboat? Unprecedented! I can pay no such fee! This is half my income for the evening!"

The official acquiesced smilingly. "The fee was calculated upon such a basis. In this ambiguous world, a concept so clear and clean as 'half' is absolutely refreshing."

Gassoon could hardly wait for morning. Before dawn he ordered all sails set and sheeted home, though they hung limp as bags in the silver calm. At last majestic Phaedra appeared and projected a band of orange-red light across the water. At this moment the air stirred and shivered the river with cat's-paws. Sails flapped and filled; hawsers were thrown clear; the vessel shouldered sluggishly out upon the water, barely maintaining way against the current. Both to exercise the bullocks and to make better speed, Zamp ordered the stern wheel into motion, to incur a lambent glare from Gassoon, who resented any encroachment upon his authority.

The Vissel, now sensibly less ample, began to meander. Back, forth, around, about, with the yards hauled hard about first on one reach, then the other, with the stern wheel dutifully thrashing backwater. The banks supported a wonderful variety of trees and shrubs. Enormous black-trunked mallows held aloft clouds of pale green foam; below clustered ink-trees, whortleberry thickets, weeping willows, an occasional giant tamarisk with a trunk twenty feet in diameter and branches crusted over with glittering white tree-barnacles.

During the afternoon the river swept around a group of ancient volcanic necks; a good source, according to the *River Index*, of pyrite crystals. On the bank a company of nomads watched the ship pass by. They sat motionless on long-legged black horses, performing no salutes, uttering no sounds: a sinister and unnerving immobility. Zamp, studying the group through Gassoon's spyglass, could not identify them. He took note of their swarthy skins, pointed jaws and chins, strange black hats with high sharp peaks and long, flaring earflaps pulled low over blazing black eyes: the faces of malign mythical creatures, redolent of musk and licorice and aromatic smoke.

Gassoon, in waspish annoyance, came up behind Zamp and took the spyglass. "I prefer that you do not use my instruments, Master Zamp; they are delicate and valuable."

Zamp sighed but made no retort. Gassoon studied the nomads. "An unsavory lot. I am glad they did not come upon us moored to the bank. Otherwise we might have suffered the fate of poor Garth Ashgale. This voyage is truly a work of foolhardy recklessness."

The nomads wheeled their mounts and were gone.

Zamp scrambled up to the crow's nest and to his relief saw the group ride south.

The day passed without incident. Shoals and sandbars made navigation difficult and Gassoon guided his ship with great care.

For two days the winds blew capriciously, then settled in strong and fair from the south; and on the fourth day after leaving Skivaree, the boat arrived at Garken, a fortified town somewhat larger than Skivaree, the terminus of caravan routes leading northeast into Lune XXIV Central and west to the Nonestic Ocean of Lunc XXII. At the docks two small cogs were moored, flying green, yellow and black gonfalons. Consulting Appendix VIII of the *River Index*, Zamp identified the colors as those of the Malou-Mandaman-Lacustrine Porterage and Transport Fellowship of the Upper Vissel.

In reference to Garken the *River Index* had little to say:

A town well fortified against the onslaughts of the Mandaman Basilisks and the tribes of the various Tinsitala nations. Garken is a caravan terminus, a staging and marketing depot for minerals, oil, slaves, fine wood, Lanteen glass, Coble musical instruments, Beynary balsam, Mandaman immortality fluid, Szegedy garnets and dozens of other commodities. The Garken market is a most colorful and stimulating sight, where fortunes in commercial stuffs change hands at a wink, a nod or the flick of a finger.

The Mercantile Syndicate maintains an efficient if stern police force, which ensures an almost unreal oasis of tranquility. At Garken are found no footpads, thieves, or truculent bravos; they are seized as soon as they appear and dealt with most definitely. For this reason Garken is a haven for just and honest men; under no circumstances attempt illicit dealings, swindling, lewdness, or violence, unless you have lost your zest for life.

Zamp read the passage with meaningful emphasis to Gassoon who glared at Zamp in indignation. "I need not fear the law-keepers of Garken! I have never performed an illicit act in my life!"

"Don't start in Garken," said Zamp. "Your years of restraint will have been wasted."

"I have no misgivings," said Gassoon. "We will advertise as usual and present performances for so long as we attract custom. I am extremely anxious to derive a profit from this so far bootless journey."

"We can spare two days," said Zamp. "No more. Time has become of the essence."

"We shall see."

Miraldra's Enchantment approached the Garken dock and tied up, attracting only scant attention. Zamp set forth his placards; the orchestra played merry tunes; the mime-girls cakewalked along the upper deck, but only a few dockside loiterers came to watch.

"Odd," said Gassoon. "Curious indeed. There is adequate population here. Surely they are not subjected to a surfeit of entertainment."

"Some trifling promotion will work wonders," said Zamp. "A parade, some music, and all will be well."

"I hope so," grumbled Gassoon. "Otherwise we'll have wasted an entire afternoon and evening."

Zamp loaded a case with tickets, formed the orchestra into a column, posted three mime-girls with placards on the right and three more on the left. Zamp jerked his arm; the band began to march along the docks, and presently started to play a lively quickstep. In alarm

Zamp signaled for silence. "Not yet! There may be restrictions against music during daylight, or some other such ordinance. Let us make certain before we commit the offense. Forward now, neatly, in good order. Girls, hold up the placards! We are selling tickets to the performance, not ogling passersby!"

Zamp led the parade through an alley out upon the central square, where booths, shops, trays and carts created a gaudy texture of color and shape and movement. A row of hostelries occupied two sides of the area; in another quarter gall-nut trees shaded a group of slave pens, some empty, others occupied. Directly opposite a great gate in the massive black brick wall framed a view across the steppe.

Zamp halted his company, which already was attracting attention. Nearby stood a tall, dark-haired man with a sallow complexion, sagging jowls and a vulpine nose, which combined to produce a markedly saturnine expression. His armor of polished black bamboo staves and his complicated leather hat of a dozen tucks and folds seemed to indicate an official status, and Zamp approached him, confident of obtaining accurate information.

"We are strangers at Garken," said Zamp. "In fact, we have just arrived aboard the showboat *Miraldra's Enchantment*, and wish to advertise our entertainment. Will we violate local ordinances by playing music and making an announcement?"

"Not at all," declared the man in the black armor. "I can speak with authority on this score, inasmuch as I am one of the magistrates."

"In that case," said Zamp, "I wish to allow you the privilege of buying the first ticket sold in Garken, at the trifling cost of half a groat."

The magistrate considered a moment, then said, "Certainly; in fact I will buy four such tickets." From his pouch he brought a tablet of papers an inch on a side, and used a small instrument to stamp a black sigil on one of these papers, which he then handed to Zamp. "Two groats, I believe, is the correct sum."

Zamp looked dubiously at the trifle of paper. "Under the circumstances, I would prefer to be paid in solid iron."

"The token is equivalent to iron," stated the magistrate in a definite voice. "It is redeemable in goods anywhere in Garken; this is the basis upon which we do business."

"If so, the concept is most ingenious," said Zamp. "Can this paper be exchanged for two groats of iron, and if so, where?"

"Notice the large structure of black brick yonder." The magistrate pointed a finger long and white as to rival any of Gassoon's. "That is the bank where all tokens such as these are cleared."

"In that case, I thank you, both for the information and your custom," said Zamp. He signaled the orchestra which at once broke into a merry tune. The mimegirls, after arranging the placards, performed an intricate dance of twirls, hops, swings and knee-bends. Spectators gathered to watch and Zamp, from time to time interrupting the music and dancing, proclaimed the quality of the entertainment to be offered that very evening aboard *Miraldra's Enchantment*. He sold a satisfactory number of tickets, all purchased with stamped squares of paper.

Agitated signals from under the gall-nut trees attracted Zamp's attention. His curiosity aroused, Zamp walked over to the slave pens. There, constrained behind a bamboo fence, he found Garth Ashgale and various members of his company.

Zamp looked gravely through the bamboo bars. "Master Ashgale, I am surprised to find you at Garken!"

"We are not here of our own volition," declared Ashgale in a quivering voice. "We were captured, threatened, herded like cattle, brought here to be sold into slavery! Can you imagine such a state of affairs? Our delight and relief at the sight of you is frankly undescribable!"

"A familiar face in a strange land," said Zamp, "is always pleasant to see. Please excuse me; I must sell tickets for the evening's performance."

Zamp returned to the orchestra, where he delivered another announcement and sold almost a hundred tickets.

Garth Ashgale continued to make urgent gestures, and Zamp at last returned to the slave pens. "Master Ashgale, were you signaling to me?"

"Yes indeed! How soon can you get us out of these pens? We are anxious to bathe and take a decent meal!"

Zamp smiled ruefully. "You exaggerate my abilities. I can do nothing for you."

Garth Ashgale leaned back aghast. "You can't intend to leave us here?"

"I have no other choice."

"But surely you can make some sort of settlement with the slave-dealer!"

Zamp gave his head a regretful shake. "I have no need for so many slaves, even if I could pay for them."

After a moment Ashgale said coldly, "If you can extricate us from this fix, your iron will be definitely and gratefully refunded."

"I have no iron," said Zamp. "Everything I owned went down at Port Whant. Perhaps there is divine justice, after all."

"Well then, what of Master Gassoon?"

Zamp thoughtfully pulled at his goatee. "I can make

a single suggestion. We lack four bullocks, but surely you would not care to occupy the stalls and work the capstans?''

Ashgale heaved a deep breath. "If that is how it must be—we accept."

Zamp sauntered to the offices of the slave-dealer, a portly man in a dark red cloak, who gave Zamp a cordial greeting. "How may I assist you?"

"In a week or so," said Zamp, "I may be in a position to sell you a dozen items. What do you pay per head?"

"Much depends upon the item itself; I can quote no exact figure until I inspect the merchandise."

"For purposes of rough comparison, let us say that they resemble that group yonder."

"Those are utility-grade, for which I pay fifteen groats a head. They have poor durability and are not much in demand."

"Indeed!" said Zamp. "I had no idea slaves went so cheap. Your selling price then would be what?"

The slave-dealer pursed his lips. "I might accept forty groats apiece. But are you selling or buying?"

"Today, if the price were within reason, I might be buying. I could offer no more than twenty groats per head."

The slave-dealer's hooded eyes flew wide in shock. "How can anyone run his business at a loss? Please be serious."

Eventually the dealer agreed to a price of twenty-six and a half groats, to make the final sum an even five hundred groats. "Now, as to payment," said Zamp, "I have here some certified paper tendered me by the folk of Garken, to the value of sixty-three groats, which I now transfer to you, to leave a total of four hundred and twenty-seven groats." He opened his case of tickets. "I pay you therefore eight hundred and fifty-four half-groat vouchers, which are similar to the certified papers of Garken—notice the official symbol of the great showboat *Miraldra's Enchantment*. They may be exchanged at the gangplank for admission to a performance, and are valuable until redeemed."

The slave-trader inspected the tickets which Zamp had tendered. "I am somewhat puzzled as to the function of these vouchers. Are they redeemable in iron?"

"In iron, if Master Gassoon so elects, or some other valuable commodity, such as admission to a performance of the drama *Macbeth*. If you choose, you may profit by selling these vouchers for double their face value to folk fresh off the steppes."

"Very well. The slaves are yours. At such a price I can make you no warranties."

"I must take my chances," said Zamp. "I will need a rope to tie them neck to neck to prevent their escape."

"Escape? To where? Still, yonder is a stout cord which will serve your needs."

Zamp led the erstwhile slaves back to the showboat, with the orchestra and mime-girls marching behind. The group filed up the gangplank and out upon the main deck where Garth Ashgale spoke in a trembling voice. "Apollon Zamp, in the past we have had our small differences, but today you have done a generous deed. Be certain that I for one will never forget your action!"

"Nor I!" declared Alpo, the chief acrobat of Zamp's old troupe. "Three cheers for Apollon Zamp, the most excellent fellow of all!"

"In due course," said Garth Ashgale. "Now I am too hungry and weak even to cheer. Remove this cord, Master Zamp; I am truly anxious for a bath, clean garments, a good supper, and then: absolute relaxation!"

"Not so fast," said Zamp with a grim smile. "Certain events along the Lant River and at the Green Star Inn are still fresh in my mind.''

"Come now, friend Zamp!" said Ashgale, "I, for one, am willing to let bygones be bygones."

"In due course, but first things first. In assuming your indentures I have paid out a substantial sum."

"Of course! We recognize the debt," said Garth Ashgale heartily. "Each pledges his share of reimbursement!"

"Very good," said Zamp. "You may now write me an irrevocable promissory note and bank draft for one thousand groats of iron; then each of the others will pay you his share, in accordance with this pledge."

Garth Ashgale began a vociferous protest, but Zamp quelled him with a gesture. "It goes without saying that until I receive the iron into my hands, the indenture holds firm, and all must work at the capstans."

"This is bitter news," said Garth Ashgale. "Your mercy has an acrid flavor."

Zamp started to make a cold retort, but was interrupted by Gassoon's strident voice: "Master Zamp, what is the reason for this incursion?"

"One moment." Zamp summoned the boatswain. "Take these folk down to the orlop; see to it that they do not stray to other sections of the ship."

The boatswain led the group away and Zamp joined Gassoon on the quarterdeck. "Perhaps you can explain these peculiar acts?" demanded Gassoon.

"Naturally. Did you not recognize Garth Ashgale and his troupe? I discovered them in the slave pens!"

Gassoon looked askance at Zamp. "And how, lacking funds, did you liberate them? I hope by neither violence nor fraud?"

Zamp spoke in a voice of cool superiority. "Lacking funds, I used persuasiveness and resource."

Gassoon clutched his head, so that tufts of white hair protruded past his fingers. "These words have an ominous sound!"

"The arrangements are perfectly straightforward," said Zamp with quiet dignity. "The slave-dealer has in effect been appointed our ticket agent. I made a most satisfactory arrangement with him."

Gassoon seemed to become limp. In a metallic voice he asked, "What are the details of this transaction?"

"I allotted him a certain number of tickets in full payment for his fees and charges."

Gassoon groaned. "How many tickets?"

"Eight hundred and fifty-four, to be exact."

"Eight hundred and fifty-four tickets! Must we play to three full houses for no return whatever?"

"Not necessarily," said Zamp. "The agent has several options. He can sell the tickets at a profit, or distribute them to his friends, or even redeem them here for iron."

Gassoon cried out in his most nasal tones, "I should pay iron for my own tickets? Inconceivable! I possess no such sum!"

"It will never come to that," said Zamp. "The situation has many advantages. Master Ashgale and his comrades have volunteered to do the work of the missing bullocks; they will also reimburse us when we return to Coble. How can we help but profit?"

Gassoon threw his hands into the air and stamped away to his office.

The evening's performance was poorly attended. Present were the slave-dealer, the magistrate, those others who had paid for their tickets in certified paper, thirty who paid at the gangplank with stamped paper squares, and perhaps a dozen others who presumable had obtained their tickets from the slave-dealer.

Gassoon glumly surveyed the empty seats. "At this rate we must remain here two weeks, playing two performances a day—for nothing."

"Hardly feasible," said Zamp. "Perhaps . . ." He paused, to pull thoughtfully at his goatee.

"Perhaps what?"

Before Zamp could explain, the magistrate and the slave-dealer approached. "An excellent performance, if somewhat macabre and dreary," declared the magistrate. "What is tomorrow's program?"

"The same," said Zamp.

The slave-dealer shook his head in displeasure. "I can sell no tickets to such a despondent affair. Here at Garken we prefer frivolity, merriment, even a bit of ribaldry, if done in good taste. I think that I will exchange these vouchers for their value in iron."

Gassoon raised his eyes to the sky. Zamp said suavely, "The vouchers are similar to your certified paper; they must be redeemed at the bank."

The slave-dealer started to expostulate, but the magistrate said, "That is reasonable enough. Who would risk the consequences of fraud for a paltry few groats of iron?"

"Undoubtedly no one," replied the slave-dealer, "but redemption day at the bank is six months away!"

"What!" cried Gassoon in wrath. "Those bits of stamped paper paid in at the gangplank window cannot be redeemed for six months?"

"Owing to the special circumstances," said the magistrate, "I will request the bank official to redeem both the certified paper and those vouchers issued on behalf of this vessel tomorrow morning. You need not fear for your iron; at Garken we are rigidly meticulous. We dare not be otherwise."

The magistrate and the slave-dealer departed. Zamp and Gassoon looked at each other. Zamp said, "Our recourse is clear and obvious."

Gassoon for once agreed with Zamp. He summoned the boatswain: "Bullocks to the capstans. Sheet home all sails, then throw off the hawsers. We depart Garken instantly."

Chapter 13

The winds blew cool and steady out of the south; stars were revealed, then obscured by moving wisps of cloud. By a near-clairvoyant feel for the loom of the low banks, the crew of *Miraldra's Enchantment* navigated the brimming river.

At midnight the winds failed. The bullocks worked two capstans, while Garth Ashgale and his troupe, bitterly protesting, thrust at the bars of the third, and the vessel continued to thrust north.

At dawn wind once more filled the sails and the stern wheel was lifted from the water. Halfway through the morning six horsemen came pounding from the south along the east bank of the river, to shout and wave their arms toward the ship. Gassoon prudently hugged the west bank and pretended to ignore the gesticulations. The horsemen at last became discouraged and turned disconsolately back toward the south. Zamp, watching through the spyglass, thought to recognize the portly shape of the slave-dealer, although a cowl shadowed his features.

"We are well clear of Garken," Zamp told Gassoon. "The natives of the place are petty and humorless; they would stop at nothing to gain an advantage."

"Nevertheless," growled Gassoon, "my reputation

for integrity, which I have jealously guarded, has now been tarnished.''

"Not necessarily," said Zamp. "The Garken bank may decide to treat our tickets as valid tokens of exchange, in which case no one is the loser.''

Late the following day the ship approached Massacre Bend, regarding which the *River Index* had nothing whatever to say. Gassoon wanted to play a performance or two in order to repair his finances; Zamp suspected that riders from Garken might have preceded the ship to Massacre Bend, with possibly unpleasant consequences; and the two conducted a lively discussion.

The argument was rendered moot as Massacre Bend came into view: a town dilapidated and deserted. Gassoon took his vessel close by the broken docks and examined the ruins through his spyglass. He saw only what might have been furtive movement in the shadows. Massacre Bend was clearly not a propitious location at which to stage a performance, and *Miraldra's Enchantment* sailed on.

The countryside had become a vast prairie. The Vissel River sprawled across the land like a gigantic sentient organism, soft and sluggish. *Miraldra's Enchantment* moved like a boat in a quiet dream, under the softest of sunny blue skies. On several occasions nomad bands showed themselves, to stare silently, or sometimes to ride along the shore hallooing and howling and waving their hats.

The *River Index* no longer offered pertinent information, although the chart tentatively located several towns: Prairie View, Idanthus, Port Venable and Castle Banoury. Gassoon insisted upon a halt at Prairie View, despite Zamp's apprehension in regard to envoys from Garken. The town was little more than a dock, a warehouse and a huddle of farmsteads; nevertheless *Macbeth* was played before an appreciative audience and Gassoon took great satisfaction within the admission receipts, so much so that he wished to lay over several days. Zamp, however, interposed his veto, citing the press of time.

On the day after leaving Prairie View a band of nomads appeared on the bank, watched a few moments, then galloped upstream with an air of purpose which Zamp considered sinister. Gassoon, engrossed in a discussion of poetry with Damsel Blanche-Aster, scoffed aside Zamp's forebodings. Two hours later *Miraldra's Enchantment*, rounding a bend in the river, encountered a fleet of a dozen coracles manned by these same nomads, armed with bows and arrows, axes and grappling hooks.

Zamp, far from being reassured by Gassoon's confidence, had put the ship's company on the alert, and now defense procedures were instantly effectuated. Arrow guards were raised to protect the helmsman and the drive capstans, at which the bullocks already were harnessed. On the foredeck Zamp aimed the howitzer of cemented glass fiber and applied a match to the fuse; the howitzer belched a charge of pebbles at the coracles, destroying three. Ashgale and his troupe were posted around the gunwales with orders to dislodge whatever grapples were flung aboard. The crew meanwhile manned the port and starboard catapults, to fling bags of volatile oil out among the coracles. Wads of burning waste then ignited the oil slick, to create an almost explosive curtain of fire. The would-be assailants screamed in despair, dived into the river and swam ashore. Zamp reloaded the howitzer and discharged it at the three coracles still floating, and almost as soon as it had started the attack was repelled.

Gassoon grudgingly acknowledged the efficacy of Zamp's measures, but wondered if Zamp had not been precipitate. "Conceivably they could have been warned off by an announcement or a display of some sort. I deplore taking lives in so wanton a fashion."

"On the other hand," Zamp pointed out, "there will be just so many fewer bloodthirsty ruffians to attack us on our return trip."

Gassoon muttered under his breath and stalked off to his office.

An hour later a dead calm fell over the prairie. Clouds boiled down from the north, where the Mandaman Mountains now loomed vaguely. Lightning thrashed at the passive land right and left, then came a pelting of cold rain. Five minutes later the storm fled off to all directions as if a great fist had struck down upon it. The sky opened and gentle breezes blew *Miraldra's Enchantment* upstream.

In late afternoon a small town appeared on the eastern shore. Checking the chart, Zamp declared the town to be Idanthus. In the absence of information, Zamp would have proceeded discreetly past, but Gassoon insisted on halting for the night, not only to stage a performance and thus benefit the exchequer, but also to be spared the danger of anchoring overnight in midstream.

Against these arguments Zamp could pose only a mood of generalized uneasiness which Gassoon derided. *Miraldra's Enchantment* eased off sheets and slid sidewise across the current against the Idanthus dock.

A crowd of Idanthus immediately appeared: a sturdy folk with ruddy complexions, blonde hair, and candid open countenances. The children especially were charming and threw flowers up on the deck of the vessel.

When Gassoon stepped forth to introduce himself and his ship, the Idanthans greeted him with enthusiasm; *Miraldra's Enchantment*, so they declared, was the first showboat they had ever seen; indeed, vessels of any sort were infrequent.

Zamp's misgivings were disarmed by the cordiality of the welcome, and it seemed as if the entire population of the town attended the evening's performance, paying in cold, honest iron, to Gassoon's satisfaction.

The drama was warmly received, to such an extent that after the final curtain Gassoon was prompted to step out on the stage. "Thank you for your enthusiasm; it is most gratifying. I truly believe that you, the perceptive citizens of this fair town, have fully comprehended what we sought to convey."

Smilingly Gassoon held up his hand to the shouts from the audience of "Again! Again!"

"Tonight we are tired and must rest, but if there are folk of the town who have missed tonight's presentation, I see no reason why we should not stage another performance tomorrow morning, before, regretfully, we take our departure from this delightful community!"

At last the audience departed the ship, and Gassoon gratefully counted the proceeds of the evening into his strongbox.

In the morning it seemed as if the town had succumbed to a mood of festival. Children had woven ropes of flax-whisk and bobadil blossoms with which they festooned the vessel: round about, bow to stern, port and starboard; and they wound so much foliage into the stern when that Zamp became concerned that navigation might be impeded.

Gassoon, wearing a festive jacket of maroon weltcloth over his usual black trousers, exclaimed to Zamp, "At last, what I had almost despaired to find: a truly enthusiastic and whole-hearted community. I laugh to recall your dire forebodings!"

"No doubt," said Zamp. "Time presses; let us get the performance over and done with."

An elder of the town approached Gassoon. "Naturally I cannot control the management of your affairs, but last night we spent iron accumulated across several years. We have no more; still—"

Zamp said smoothly, "You may pay in fresh produce and fodder for our beasts."

The elder scratched his head. "We lack fodder, and as for garden stuffs, would you want to pull the food from the throats of your friends? Let the performance begin! We will worry about prices and profits some other time. Is it after all so important? We are planning a great feast in your honor three days from now. All will provide their best; all will eat and drink their fill. We are ordering in six tuns of mead, shillicks and pechavies to be roasted, loads of sweetmeats: the event will transcend all others in the history of Idanthus!"

Zamp remarked, "Such affairs are expensive; how will you pay if you have spent all your iron?"

"One or another means will surely be found. We consider forthright generosity the prime virtue; at Idanthus no one shirks or holds back what he has. It is mean and niggling for a person to hoard a great store of iron when his friend lacks, or cannot make payment!" For a moment the elder's eyes flashed and he seemed almost indignant.

"A noble sentiment," Gassoon remarked thoughtfully.

"In the meantime, on with the performance! Let us enjoy each instant of our all-too-fugitive lives!"

"Very well," said Zamp. "One last performance, then we must be on our way, as we have important business elsewhere!"

The elder expressed shock and dismay. "Surely you would not leave us on the eve of the great feast!"

"We have no choice," said Zamp. "Our business is urgent."

"Yes," said Gassoon, "urgent indeed. Very, very urgent."

"This news will sadden everyone," said the elder. "We had looked forward to enjoying your entire repertory, rather than just the rather melancholy affair of last night."

"That is the only piece we know," said Zamp. "We are presenting it again today. The curtain is ready to rise; please be seated."

Again *Macbeth*, a production perhaps overly grim for such a merry occasion, especially since Zamp had excised certain of those spectacles introduced for the very purpose of enlivening the drama. The applause of the Idanthans, while hearty and unstinted, lacked the feverish enthusiasm of the night before. At the final curtain Gassoon came forth on the stage.

"We are sorry but now we must leave. Our visit has been all too brief, still—"

From the audience came shouts: "Don't go, don't go!" "You must stay and entertain us always!" "Another performance; play us another piece from your vast repertory!"

Gassoon smiled and held up his hands to quell the cries. "All this is most flattering, but we must depart. Will you be so good as to remove the garlands and flower ropes so that our vessel may proceed?"

"The garlands are known as 'Strands of Love,' " said the elder. "No one would dare to break them."

Zamp came forth on the stage. "We are overwhelmed by your enthusiasm and generosity, and have no choice but to submit. We now present another performance: the majestic tragedy *Macbeth*."

"*Macbeth* again?" demanded the elder rather querulously.

"There are immense depths of meaning to the drama," said Zamp. "The work is an inexhaustible treasure!"

Again *Macbeth*, and Zamp on this occasion excised the singing and wailing which gave the witch scenes their pungency, and all the soliloquies were delivered twice. Several members of the audience, with affairs elsewhere, decided to depart, only to find that the gangplank had been drawn up so that they were compelled to remain.

At the end of the drama, Zamp appeared on the stage. "We cannot let ourselves be outdone in liberality or effusiveness! Do not stir from your seats; we intend to present our performance again, at no cost. So now to Act 1, Scene 1. Please attend the sublimity of the language, and also the profundity of the sentiments!"

Macbeth was now played with the witches in ordinary costumes, and sitting in chairs like tired char women; soliloquies were repeated twice, and the orchestral accompaniment was reduced to the music of one belp-horn, a thunder-machine and brattle-drums. The curtain dropping on the last scene drew back immediately upon Act 1, Scene 1, and the three witches on the heath. The audience seemed somewhat restless, and many rose from their seats to stand in the aisles, so that Zamp, pausing in one of his soliloquies, came to the front of the stage.

"Friends!" called Zamp. "Please attend our performance! We are giving our best, and we intend to do so without cessation!"

"Be so good as to lower the gangplank!" called the elder. "I have business ashore!"

"We can only remain at Idanthus so long as you give

us your enthusiastic attention," Zamp said, "so please resume your seat."

"Play something else! We have had enough of this portentous drama."

"We play only *Macbeth*; that is all we know."

"In that case you must leave Idanthus," exclaimed the elder with sudden energy, "and take *Macbeth* with you!"

Fifty miles north of Idanthus the Vissel entered a region of rocky hills and green meadows, shadowed under Doric elms, black sentinel syrax, gray-green and silver tremblants: a landscape as soft and delightful as lost Arcadia, but eerily quiet so that even the wind disappeared and the river flowed like syrup. Gassoon ordered the stern wheel into operation; the bullocks, Garth Ashgale and his artistes were all pressed into service, and the vessel continued up the brimming river. Zamp sat on the quarterdeck sipping wine, dividing his attention between the landscape and Garth Ashgale thrusting at the capstan.

Where a tall, dark forest came down to the river stood a town of blue- and red-painted timber, which Zamp assumed to be Port Venable. In the absence of wind and with night close at hand, Gassoon decided to dock and stage a performance in the hope of earning iron. Zamp made another uneasy protestation. "We know nothing in regard to these folk, and we have had one or two experiences along the way to teach us caution."

Gassoon inspected the town through his spyglass. "I see nothing alarming. The folk appear of normal stature and show neither fangs, tails nor horns. Your character, Apollon Zamp, is marred by a certain paltriness of spirit, a diffused universal distrust which I truly deplore."

Zamp was at a loss for response, and Gassoon stalked off to instruct the quartermaster. *Miraldra's Enchantment* veered across the river and eased against the dock of the town.

A grave and somber gathering came forth to listen to Gassoon's announcement: "This is the wonderful showboat *Miraldra's Enchantment*, and we are prepared to present for your enjoyment that classic of medieval Earth *Macbeth*. But first I must inquire as to your local regulations and how they apply to us: for instance, do you charge a dock fee?"

A spokesman from the folk of Port Venable, as the town was known, assured Gassoon that no extraordinary regulations prevailed. "However, it is considered polite practice to distribute complimentary tickets to the town officials and their families."

Gassoon pulled at his long chin. "And how many are these town officials?"

"About thirty."

"And how many persons are included in the average family?"

"As we reckon kinship, the family group normally includes about eleven or twelve persons."

"Interesting!" said Gassoon. "The folk of Port Venable evidently enjoy close and cordial family relationships."

"We do indeed."

Gassoon, surveying the town, estimated its total population to be approximately four hundred. "We will make a concession even more generous," he said in a grand voice. "Our admission fee is ordinarily one groat; tonight, rather than distribute complimentary tickets, we will reduce this price by half, in order that everyone of Port Venable may profit, rich and poor alike."

"This is good to hear!" declared the Port Venable

citizen. "Such expansive goodwill is rarely encountered nowadays!"

Gassoon immediately put the tickets on sale and Zamp repaired to a dockside tavern. Here he learned that Bottomless Lake lay still a hundred miles north across a robber-infested wilderness.

"The region is home for all the outcasts of Soyvanesse," stated his informant. "The worst of all is Baron Banoury, who inhabits a castle at the Mandaman gate. For a ship like yours he will demand an enormous toll: two hundred groats at least. If you refuse to pay, he will drop rocks upon your vessel as you pass through the chasm."

Zamp blew out his cheeks in dismay. "This is a consistent policy?"

"As consistent as the flow of beer—from vat, through mug and gut, to trough."

"Throdorus Gassoon, my associate, will not submit gracefully to this toll," said Zamp. "He might refuse to traverse the Mandaman gate, or even so much as approach."

"That, of course, is his option."

The evenings's presentation went flawlessly and Gassoon received numerous compliments upon the deftness and vivacity of his troupe. Zamp stood close at hand. Someone remarked: "An absolute disgrace that Baron Banoury—"

Zamp quickly interrupted, "Yes, we hope to make this voyage again with a new repertory." Again, when with a rueful shudder someone said: "The castles of old Earth, such as Glamis, were no doubt grim, but when compared to the castle of Baron—" Zamp said quickly, "On our return down the Vissel we will stop again at Port Venable for a longer stay."

"Yes, to be sure," said Gassoon, somewhat bemused. "But who is this baron?"

Zamp touched Gassoon's elbow. "Excuse me, Master Gassoon, but while you accept the congratulations of these good folk, Damsel Blanche-Aster and I are going ashore to take a glass or two at the tavern."

"Not so fast!" roared Gassoon. "There are certain matters I wish to discuss with her, and your presence would not be convenient for either of us. You may go off to drink with Viliweg or another of your cronies." And making his apologies to the townsfolk, Gassoon strode off to find Damsel Blanche-Aster.

At dawn *Miraldra's Enchantment* cast off from the Port Venable dock and set its sails to a gusty wind, the last gasp of the monsoon. Zamp took Ethan Quaner the ship's engineer, Baltrop the carpenter and several other men into the hold under that area of the deck where the audience sat and ordered a modification of the jackscrews by which an unruly audience could be tilted over the side.

Gassoon presently became aware of the pounding and thumping of the workmen and demanded an explanation. Zamp informed the gaunt shipmaster that certain braces and stanchions were being renewed. "Perhaps you should go down into the hold and stay there while the work is being completed. I would do so myself except that—," here Zamp glanced across the quarterdeck to where Damsel Blanche-Aster stood watching the shore slide past, "—I have other affairs in mind."

Gassoon noted the direction of Zamp's gaze. "The task is quite well within your capabilities," he said frigidly.

"As you wish."

The day advanced, and the countryside became rough and wild; ahead the Mandaman Palisades lay directly athwart the course of the river. At various times during the day bands of wild-looking men appeared on the bank to stare in wonder at the passing vessel, and when dusk arrived, rather than anchor and risk an attack, Gassoon chose to continue up the river, steering by starlight and the sheen of the water.

The next morning the Mandaman Palisades jutted high into the northern sky, and at noon the great gorge by which the Vissel drained the Bottomless Lake had become manifest. A bare half-mile short of this gorge, seeming to grow from the very substance of a low crag, appeared a castle, consisting of a keep, six turrets of varying heights, and a wall with a small timber portal.

As *Miraldra's Enchantment* appeared, a black pinnace put out from a dock and hailed the showboat. "Ahoy aboardship! Back your sails, drop anchor and prepare to pay the toll required by Baron Banoury!"

Gassoon threw his head back in outrage. "Toll? Stuff and nonsense. We are bound for Mornune!"

"No matter. Lower a ladder."

Gassoon sullenly signaled the boatswain, who dropped an accommodation ladder over the side. A burly man in black and purple armor clambered aboard. Gassoon came forward. "What is this absurd talk of toll? We are here at the invitation of King Waldemar; we are definitely exempted from expense."

"Protests are useless. Waldemar himself would be obligated to pay. Baron Banoury controls the Gate. If you wish to pass you must pay him five hundred groats."

Gassoon seemed to strangle on his words. "We will pay nothing of the sort! This is extortion, sheer and simple! I prefer to turn about and proceed downstream the way we came!"

Zamp stepped forward. "You are the Baron Banoury?"

"I am the Knight Sir Arban, Master of the Guard, Warden of the Gate and Chief Toll-taker."

"As you see, this is a showboat," said Zamp. "We are bound for the Festival at Mornune; and we are unable to pay so large a toll."

"Then you may not pass."

"Perhaps you will allow us to present our entertainment for the amusement of yourself, Baron Banoury, and the ladies and gentlemen of his court, in lieu of toll?"

"Aha! We cannot let you pass so cheaply!"

"How much toll will you then remit?"

Sir Arban considered. "Subject to the approval of Banoury, fifty groats. You also must serve refreshments."

Gassoon emitted a groan of rage. "You demand too much."

"In any event," said Zamp reasonably, "we will present our magnificent drama before these people and perhaps blunt the edge of their avarice."

Sir Arban chuckled. "If your performance is as fanciful as your hopes, we shall spend a delightful afternoon. Take your boat, then, to the dock."

"With pleasure," said Zamp. "The entertainment will begin in precisely one hour."

Miraldra's Enchantment, holding only enough way to negate the effect of the current, eased over to the dock. Overhead loomed the castle wall, with six turrets on the sky behind. A pair of bartizans flanked the gate, from which a number of curious folk watched the approach of the showboat. As soon as hawsers had been looped over bollards and the gangplank swung out, Zamp set forth his placards, then returned aboard to assure himself as to the condition of his preparations.

Gassoon came to Zamp in quivering perturbation.

"Why have not the benches been arranged? Haskel tells me that you gave absolute orders to the contrary!"

"Correct. I know how to deal with this extortionate baron, and hopefully I will curb his insolence. After all, are we not Throdorus Gassoon and Apollon Zamp, famous ship-masters and kings of the river?"

Gassoon's prominent teeth showed in a sneering grimace. "If we are thrust into a dungeon we can so solace ourselves. No, Zamp, as usual you are capering off in pursuit of a chimera. Our best hope to avoid an extortionate toll lies in politeness, cooperation and affability. If these are insufficient then there is no choice for it; we must return downstream to Coble. Haskel! Set out the benches! Drape them with decorative buntings!"

"Perhaps you are right," said Zamp, "but I wish to show you an important note in the *River Index*." He conducted Gassoon aft to the door of the office, politely stood back to allow Gassoon's entry, then closed the door upon the ship-master's incredulous bellow. Zamp wedged the door shut with a pair of poles against a nearby bulkhead, these poles having been measured, cut and arranged for just such a purpose that very morning.

Ignoring Gassoon's strident calls, Zamp returned to the main deck, and reversed the order to Haskel. Five minutes later the gate through the lowering wall swung ajar; down the road moved a splendid procession, led by a pair of heralds in lavender hose and gray doublets. They stepped to a ceremonial, long-gaited slow march and carried aloft a pair of black and purple gonfalons. Behind sauntered the gentlefolk of Baron Banoury's court, the noblemen armored in cuirasses and morions of purple, green, dark red, or black membrane, lacquered and polished and decked with silver rosettes and spangles. The ladies wore embroidered gowns, soft leather shoes, hats of the most ornate and elaborate concepts imaginable. Several of the older knights, dour and sardonic, wore suits of rich black velvet with tall, black, narrow-brimmed hats. Many of these folk affected pomanders attached to their wrists by cords of braided silk, which they often raised delicately to their noses, as if the air off the river carried an odor too fresh and harsh to be borne.

Behind the aristocrats marched a company of vastly different sort, composed of burly men in purple and black uniforms, armed with halberds and swords. Their faces, round, heavy and blunt as porridge pots, were so alike, with compressed features, small eyes squinting, mouths down-slanting, as to suggest a single inbred clan. They marched with unsmiling precision, with a kind of mindless zest in their manner of stamping their feet upon the ground.

The heralds paused at the gangplank; the noble-folk inspected the placards with indolent interest, and Zamp thought to identify Baron Banoury: a portly middle-aged man of no great stature, with curly ginger-colored hair and moustaches. His lady, even more corpulent and somewhat taller, wore her hair in an astonishing confection of puffs and spires, billows and curls.

The soldier captain blew his whistle; a squad ran up the gangplank to examine decks, stage and passages for evidence of treacherous ambuscade; discovering none, they stationed themselves in commanding positions. Baron Banoury and his entourage now boarded the vessel.

Zamp stepped forward. "The personnel of *Miraldra's Enchantment* welcomes Baron Banoury and his distinguished circle aboard this vessel. Our aim is to create a cordial relationship, to such an extent that Baron Banoury will waive his usual toll. To this end, we intend to present a merry program of entertainments and musical fancies."

"I am Baron Banoury," declared the portly man. "I appreciate your sentiments, but I must insist upon my customary levy, lest a detrimental precedent be set."

Zamp made a gracious motion. "Sir, I sympathize with your dilemma; still, to pay the toll would result in our impoverishment; in fact, I doubt if we could muster any such sum."

Baron Banoury gestured toward the Mandaman Palisades. "Raise your eyes to the heights. What do you see along the skyline?"

Zamp inspected the row of contrivances. "They resemble gantrys on frames; there is even a macabre suggestion of the gibbet."

Baron Banoury nodded. "I point out these devices merely to indicate how seriously I regard financial delinquency. Whoever comes this far must pay."

Zamp bowed his head. "You will of course allow us a generous remittance for our performance?"

"We shall see, we shall see," Baron Banoury indicated the deck. "Why have not seats been arranged for our comfort?"

"Our introductory number is a pavane. Lords and ladies frequently enjoy pacing the figures." Zamp turned to the stage. "Let the music begin! Baron Banoury wishes to dance!"

The curtain slid aside to reveal the orchestra, which commenced upon a measured and dignified tune.

Baron Bancoury showed no inclination to dance, but with his company moved forward to inspect the orchestra. Zamp raised his hand. The music stopped short. In the hold the boatswain and Baltrop the carpenter swung mallets to dislodge a pair of posts. The deck split in the middle and fell apart, precipitating Baron Banoury and his party into the opening. Bullocks turned the capstans; ropes tautened; blocks squeaked; up from the hold was hoisted a cargo net laden with the persons of Baron Banoury, his companions and their ladies. The company of guards watched in stupefaction, then gave hoarse calls of outrage. They charged the quarterdeck, to be met by a jet of water which washed them over the side.

"Slip the hawsers!" ordered Zamp. "Make all sail! Full power to the stern wheel! We are about to negotiate the famous Mandaman Gate!"

Miraldra's Enchantment slid upstream. Zamp gave his attention to the occupants of the net, now dangling twenty feet above the deck from the end of the cargo boom. He peered among the compressed miscellany of arms, legs, buttocks, contorted faces, trying to locate Baron Banoury, and finally found him at the very bottom of the net with his corpulent spouse sitting on his neck, herself in little better condition, with a leg apparently belonging to Sir Arban ungallantly thrust across her shoulder and an unidentifiable elbow in her coiffure. The net quivered and bulged to the movement of the occupants, as those below tried to dislodge those on top. Baron Banoury, under the rump of his spouse, lacked almost all scope for movement. By bending and peering upward Zamp was able to look into Banoury's face. The position was uncomfortable and Zamp gave orders for the net to be raised and the boom swung to a more convenient angle.

To make himself heard above the objurgations, Zamp was forced to raise his voice. "I regret the necessity of so much discomfort," he assured Baron Banoury, "but, as you yourself must know, such steps often cannot be avoided."

Baron Banoury, his face congested, made an incoherent reply.

Zamp, remembering Gassoon, sent a steward to open the office. Gassoon stalked out upon the deck, to gaze wildly around. The cargo net swung; Gassoon ducked and jumped aside in consternation.

Zamp, leaning on the quarterdeck rail, said: "You are looking at Baron Banoury and his group, who will accompany us through the Mandaman Gate, and who in fact will be with us during our visit to Mornune."

Despite the successful effect of Zamp's plans, Gassoon could not restrain his reproaches, to which Zamp gave mild and reasonable replies.

The ship approached the awesome bulk of the Palisades. Crags rose sheer from the river, which across a million years had cut an astonishing chasm through the mountains.

The current slid swiftly and the boat lost headway. Gassoon ordered Garth Ashgale and his gang to the capstans to assist the bullocks, and the vessel crept foot by foot, yard by yard, up the chasm. The water ran dark, silent and heavy, striated like pulled taffy.

A mile passed. The chasm became even more constricted, and crags seemed to overhang the water. Raising his eyes, Zamp felt his head swim with vertigo. He transferred his attention to the cargo net where the inhabitants of Banoury Castle at last, after many curses and protests, had reordered their positions to allow Baron Banoury somewhat more comfort. Banoury called down to Zamp: "Lower the net; let us at least stand on the deck!"

"In due course you will be assisting with the work at the capstans. Control your impatience until then."

"You will never profit by such treachery!"

Zamp took no notice of the threat.

The walls closed in to allow a channel barely twice the width of the ship; however, instead of rushing at greater velocity, the water seemed instead to lie almost stagnant, and Zamp wondered how deep this channel must be to allow such a condition.

Miraldra's Enchantment moved easily now, swirling aside the cold dark water. Ahead the cliffs fell aside, allowing a view over calm vistas and dreaming pearl-colored sky. A few moments later the ship left the waters of the Vissel River and floated out upon Bottomless Lake.

Chapter 14

The charts which Zamp had been able to assemble at Coble offered only contradictions. One indicted Bottomless Lake to be a circular body surrounded by towering mountains; another depicted a shape like a man's outspread hand, with five crooked fjords extending from a central section. The specified dimensions were as disparate, ranging from a diameter of a hundred miles to a surface little larger than a millpond. One theorist identified Bottomless Lake as a natural vent into the viscera of an animate planet; another hypothesized a cavity created by the explosion of an ancient volcano, and cited the tortured relief of the surrounding mountains as evidence, although this view was challenged by another authority on theosophical grounds.

Zamp now lowered the cargo net and allowed Baron Banoury and his company to extricate themselves one by one, to be disarmed, relieved of pouches, jewels, metal ornaments, pomanders, flasks of scent and the like. Gassoon stood disdainfully aside during this process though he stepped forward to appraise the heap of valuables.

Zamp inquired of Baron Banoury, "What is the geography of this lake? Where lies Mornune, for instance?"

Bancoury sullenly pretended ignorance of such matters. "The town is somewhere yonder, the seat of a mean and capricious tyrant. If he takes note of me, he will feed me to his sacred owls. You might as well drown me here and now, or even better allow me the use of a small boat so that I may return to my castle."

"This is an impractical suggestion. I distinctly remember your unyielding manner and your reference to gibbets."

"You thereby condemn us all to an unpleasant end."

"Who lives forever? You should have considered these possibilities before you attempted to plunder us. You and your company may go to the starboard capstan and relieve the team of bullocks which now labors there."

"Must we toil like animals?" shouted Baron Banoury, at last overwrought. "Have you no gallantry? These ladies know nothing of such exercise!"

"It is simple enough," said Zamp. "One thrusts at the bar with all his weight until the bar moves, then he or she steps forward and repeats the act. In almost no time you will learn the skills."

Disconsolate and complaining, the erstwhile noblefolk were taken to the capstan and disposed to their duties.

Damsel Blanche-Aster, as usual, had kept remote and apart from the activity of the day. She was not now on deck and Zamp went to seek her in her cabin. By some circumstance the door stood slightly ajar; peering through the aperture Zamp observed Damsel Blanche-Aster in the act of trying on the garment which Zamp had seen once before, at the Green Star Inn: an intricately embroidered jacket, at one time an article of great elegance but now somewhat shabby and threadbare. Damsel Blanche-Aster seemed dissatisfied with her appearance, for she removed the garment and pulled a dark blue jacket over her head.

Zamp knocked at the door; Damsel Blanche-Aster gave a startled gasp and then looked forth into the corridor. "What do you wish?"

"Advice, instruction and information. We are lost upon the face of the Bottomless Lake."

Damsel Blanche-Aster wordlessly came out into the corridor and Zamp took her up to the quarterdeck. "The most eminent geographers of Lune XXIII contradict each other in regard to this remarkable body of water," said Zamp. "We cannot decide which direction to steer."

"Steer yonder." Damsel Blanche-Aster pointed to the northeast. "The lake is about forty miles long; you can just barely see the Myrmont. Below, along the Cynthiana, is Mornune."

As they spoke a long black galley appeared from the shadows under the eastern crags and thrust at great speed toward *Miraldra's Enchantment*. Zamp ordered the howitzer to be brought to bear.

Damsel Blanche-Aster counseled against any show of defiance. "This is one of King Waldemar's patrols; you need merely display your safe-conduct. By no means mention my presence!"

The galley surged across the water on thirty oars, to lay alongside the showboat. Zamp lowered the accommodation ladder and a flashing-eyed, dark-haired young officer in a handsome uniform of green, purple and black clambered aboard. "Navigation on this lake is forbidden to aliens," he declared. "We are ordered to sink all intruding vessels. Prepare to drown."

Zamp produced the safe-conduct which he had earned so long ago at Lanteen; the officer scrutinized the metal with care. "You are Apollon Zamp?"

"I am."

"And this ship is *Miraldra's Enchantment*?"

"The legend under the bows speaks for itself."

"One moment." The officer went to the ladder and called down into the galley: "Pass up the ledger of current business." While waiting he said to Zamp, "You must excuse our severity; the country swarms with folk of unspeakable character, including insurrectionists, political and moral deviates, and persons of low caste. We tolerate no such folk in our realm, except by force of such an instrument as you yourself bear."

"Your remark admits of varying interpretations," said Zamp haughtily. "Since I am not an insurrectionist, it would appear that you have described me as either a deviate or a person of low caste."

"Interpret my remarks as you like," said the officer. "My only concern is your positive identification." He took the ledger which had been handed up to him. He checked a symbol on Zamp's plaque and turned to a page in the ledger.

" 'Summons and invitation issued to one Apollon Zamp at the town Lanteen, that he may bring his troupe of harlequins before King Waldemar. His description is as follows: a man thus and thus . . .' " The officer scanned the description, comparing the specifics against the person of Zamp himself. "Very well; you may proceed. Bear yonder toward Mount Myr, which marks the mouth of Cynthiana Bay."

The officer returned to his galley; Zamp signaled the boatswain, who in turn chirruped to the bullocks and the companies of Garth Ashgale and Baron Banoury respectively. The capstans turned; the stern wheel pounded at the water; the ship proceeded across the lake. Zamp, idling on the quarterdeck, felt that the velocity of motion was not all that it might have been, and considered a competition between the two groups; but before he was able to formulate the terms of such a contest, a breeze dropped out of the sky to raise cat's-paws on the lake and fill the sails. Zamp halted all action at the capstans and raised the wheel from the water.

Phaedra dropped behind the palisades and night fell across the lake. Through the clear air the stars shone bright and exact, and the quartermaster steered by Ormaz the One-eyed. Two hours before midnight the breeze dwindled to a breath and the vessel ghosted across the lake, not as fast as a man might crawl.

Zamp, unable to sleep or even relax, wandered the decks and found Damsel Blanche-Aster at the bow. She gave no sign that his presence was welcome; nevertheless he joined her. For a moment the two stood in silence, looking across the water. The stars in the sky and those reflected created an all-encompassing cosmos; they might have been drifting through space.

Zamp asked politely, "Can you see the lights of Mornune?"

"They are invisible around the slant of the hillside."

"Now that you are close to home and the completion of your mission, no doubt you are exultant."

In the starlight Zamp saw her shoulders move. She muttered, "I am frightened."

After a moment Zamp said, "It is useless offering counsel; you would tell me only another fable."

Damsel Blanche-Aster laughed softly. "I have told you no fables. Half-fables, perhaps. What is to be done I must do myself." She turned to face Zamp. "Only please do not force me to act against my will!"

It was Zamp's turn to laugh sadly. "We have been through these matters a dozen times, and you have emerged intact. Why are you now concerned?"

"I mean at Mornune, or in connection with the performance. You must tolerate my whims."

Zamp shrugged. "So long as we win King Waldemar's prize."

Damsel Blanche-Aster made a half-amused, half-scornful sound. "You will not win the prize! Poor Apollon Zamp! You do not know the delicacy of Waldemar's tastes! He will sit unmoved by your hopping witches and heroic declamations!"

Zamp heaved a deep sigh. "There are no changes I can make now. . . . In all kindness, might you not have explained something of this at Coble?"

Damsel Blanche-Aster stared northward across the water. "I know nothing of kindness. Little enough has been shown to me, except by Throdorus Gassoon."

Zamp said nothing. The night air seemed suddenly chill. Damsel Blanche-Aster went on in a dull voice. "I know what you are thinking. But remember, I never pretended to be anything other than self-serving."

"Heigh-ho!" said Zamp. "So here we are at Mornune, and come what may we must play *Macbeth* for King Waldemar, even though he chokes with boredom." He turned away and walked slowly aft, leaving Damsel Blanche-Aster standing at the bow. On the quarterdeck he ordered a pot of tea from the steward and sat an hour watching the sails billow pale in the starshine and listening to the sounds of the ship.

Gassoon came from his office to stand blinking and peering. "Ah there, Zamp. You sit alone."

"This has been a difficult day."

"Most difficult. Still we have negotiated it successfully. And ahead lies tomorrow, which I hope will bring us closer to our goal."

"So I hope."

"It can hardly go otherwise," said Gassoon. "I must admit to a state of anticipation and excitement."

"We have come a long way," said Zamp. "It will be a long way back to Coble."

*   *   *

Dawn appeared in colors of pearl and white opal, from a sky ringed around with mist, and the lake shuddered to the cool light like sensitive flesh.

Miraldra's Enchantment had made little progress during the night. Zamp estimated that they now floated at the very center of the lake; and he did not care to speculate upon the black depths below. Zamp brought up a team of bullocks and his two gangs. As he watched Garth Ashgale and Baron Banoury leaning to the capstan he reflected that no matter what the eventualities of this voyage, certain memories would console him to the end of his years.

Phaedra rose into the sky. The mists dissolved; the air became clear, and ahead, plain to see, was Myrmont and the mouth of Cynthiana Bay. Across the lake darted a pair of black galleys, each mounted with rocket-launching tubes. Zamp was again forced to produce his safe-conduct and submit to an inquisition. Almost reluctantly the officers departed and Zamp was allowed to proceed.

An hour later the ship slid around the flanks of Myrmont into Cynthiana Bay. On the slopes appeared ranks of white palaces under tall dark syrax trees: the town Mornune.

A long dock of white stone fronted the lake, beside which floated a half dozen vessels. Certain of these seemed to be showboats, built to styles different from any Zamp had ever seen or known.

An esplanade ran parallel to the dock, bounded by a balustrade of carved stone. At fifty-foot intervals great urns on pedestals trailed a black and brown foliage with scarlet blossoms. Across the way shops displayed wares of many styles behind tall glass windows. Palaces occupied the slopes above, half-hidden behind the foliage of syrax, jangal, fern indigo, greenock. The dock and esplanade continued north two miles and finally disappeared around a curve of the shore. Cynthiana Bay gradually narrowed while the hills to either side dwindled and fell back; the bay became a broad river extending far off and away to the north.

The folk of Mornune passed along the esplanade in costumes of elegant simplicity. Few turned glances of more than casual curiosity toward *Miraldra's Enchantment*.

A group of four men in black and gold uniforms approached. They halted, considered the vessel in grave calculation; then one, wearing a black cap with a gold-embroidered visor, consulted the pages of a ledger. He made a sardonic comment to his fellows, and climbed the gangplank.

Zamp stepped forward to meet him. Gassoon, on the quarterdeck, watched the confrontation with a disdainful expression.

The official introduced himself. "I am the Director of Docks; be so good as to identify yourself and your ship."

In a somewhat lofty voice Zamp said "I am Master Apollon Zamp and this is my famous vessel *Miraldra's Enchantment*." For the third time Zamp produced his silver warrant. "Our home port is Coble on Surmise Bay, as you no doubt know."

The official looked up in mystification, then shrugged and, opening his ledger, checked the plaque against a set of notations. He inspected Zamp, again consulted his ledger. Finally he nodded, "Your authorization appears to be valid. I must remark, unofficially, that you arrive with the most careless and casual insouciance. The Festival of Art and Gaiety begins tomorrow."

"So long as we are not late, no great harm is done," said Zamp.

The official turned Zamp another cool glance. "Your name of course will be included upon the list of participants. Had you arrived tomorrow, your journey might have been in vain."

"We intended no disrespect," said Zamp stiffly. "The way from Coble is long. The winds at this season are undependable."

"No doubt, no doubt." The Director of Docks slapped the ledger against his thigh. "It is all one, since you have evidently arrived. You will be assigned the sixth and final place in the competition."

"Such details are of course at your discretion."

"Tomorrow morning the festival officially opens. It is recommended that you decorate your vessel in black, scarlet and gold, to honor the Dynastic Tabard."

Zamp acknowledged the advice. "We wish to attend the other presentations. I rely upon you to make the arrangements for us."

"You are allowed two places at each phase of the competition," the Director of Docks responded in an even, if somewhat metallic voice, "which begins at noon tomorrow aboard the ship *Voyuz*."

The Director of Docks performed a formal salute and took his leave. Zamp sought out Gassoon and conveyed the purport of the meeting. Gassoon, who had succumbed to a mood of depression and despondency, listened with only half an ear. "This expedition is a piece of rattlebrained tomfoolery, no more and no less. We are obviously out of our element here. These folk are caustic, cynical, hyper-civilized. They will mock our attempts at authenticity. I am not sanguine as to our chances."

"There is little time to prepare a new entertainment," said Zamp dubiously, "although I suppose—"

"No!" rasped Gassoon with sudden energy. "Let

them scoff as they see fit! I will never compromise what I consider my art, especially for the sake of gain!''

"For the sake of gain I'd compromise the art of my grandmother," muttered Zamp under his breath.

"I beg your pardon?" asked Gassoon. "What did you say?"

"Nothing of consequence. We are allowed two places at the first presentation, aboard the ship *Voyuz*. Do you choose to attend, or will you allow Damsel Blanche-Aster to go in your stead?"

"If only two places are allowed us, you shall remain aboard the ship, making ready for our show."

Damsel Blanche-Aster herself settled the argument. "I will attend none of the entertainments. You two may go together."

The swan-ship *Voyuz* had been built to lavish and opulent standards, without thought for expense, and with the most assiduous concern for comfort and convenience. The superstructure was pale sanoe wood, embellished with fretwork of intricacy upon intricacy. The audience sat on cushioned benches with a deep rose carpet underfoot and a canopy of patterned silk overhead, to shield them from the daylight.

Zamp and Gassoon boarded the craft an hour early and were conducted to back-row seats by an obsequious usher in pale green livery, and a moment later a girl in dark green tights brought two moist perfumed towels on a tray that they might refresh their faces. Both Gassoon and Zamp were impressed by the luxurious appointments of the ship, although Gassoon asserted the old-rose carpet to be a piece of sheer ostentation and a sore trial to keep clean. "How would a vessel like this look after an evening at Chist or Fudurth? Poorly indeed!''

Zamp objected to the dimensions of the stage on

technical grounds. "Sound will never project from such a cavern," he told Gassoon. "There is too much height for the breadth. We will hear only mumbling unless the artistes own the lungs and voices of sagmaws."

"A theater should be austere and unobtrusive in its decor," stated Gassoon. "A jewel shows best on a cloth of black velvet; just so should the performance enhance the theater. This luxury—," Gassoon made a scornful gesture, "—I consider sheer vulgarity."

"I doubt if we'll see anything too skillful," Zamp agreed. "Perhaps a set of erotic pantomimes, or a comedy such as my old *Cuckold's Revenge*. At least the reactions of the audience will be interesting."

"Especially those of King Waldemar, although I doubt if he will reveal himself so early in the competition."

Persons of dignified mien began to enter the chamber. Ignoring Zamp and Gassoon as if the two shipmasters failed to exist, they greeted their acquaintances with measured gestures. Seating arrangements, so Zamp noted, were governed by precise protocol, an exactitude reflected in the formality of dress. A peculiar and even somewhat bizarre discord, in Zamp's opinion, were the cockades worn by the men at the sides of their small, stiff hats: green and gold to the right, red and gold to the left. The plumes fixed into the coiffures of the ladies were similarly green and gold on the right, red and gold on the left.

A portly man in a suit of russet and orange with a black cummerbund, seated himself beside Zamp; the two entered into conversation, the newcomer identifying himself as Roald Tush, Master of the showboat *Perfumed Oliolus*. For a period the two discussed vicissitudes along the Cynthiana River as compared to those of the Lower Vissel and found many parallel circumstances. Zamp however had never encountered an audience like that among which they sat, and Tush in terms which Zamp considered astonishingly frank expressed his own lack of enthusiasm for Mornune and its population. "They are extremely difficult to please, and despite their wealth not altogether openhanded, if in fact they deign to visit your boat in the first place."

"You have verified my own instinctive judgment," said Zamp. "I have never seen folk so punctilious. Notice the precise inclination of their heads as they greet each other!"

"There is substance in the most trifling nuances of their behavior," stated Tush. "I would bore you by explaining their etiquette, but you may believe them to be a complicated and subtle folk. For instance, this audience includes princes, dukes, earls, barons and knights, each of whom must carefully graduate his conduct as he pays his respects about the room. Still, to the uninitiated, no great variance is evident."

"I admit as much," said Zamp. "How does one make a distinction? By the tilt of the cockades and feathers?"

Tush smilingly shook his head. "The green and gold symbolizes their reverence for the memory of the Doro Dynasty. These were heroic kings who defeated the Saguald Dominators, founded the kingdom of Soyvanesse, mined the Black Bog for iron and built the Magic Loom which thereupon wove the green and gold Tabard of Destiny."

"An interesting legend, to be sure. King Waldemar claims this lineage?"

"He would not dare to do so, since he lacks the green and gold Tabard which would certify such a claim. In fact, the line was broken two hundred years ago when Shimrod the Usurper drowned the Green and Gold Tabard, and the last Doro, in Bottomless Lake. Am I boring you with this historical dissertation?''

"By no means!" declared Zamp. "I am anxious to learn something of the local history, for more reasons than one. Where did the line progress after Shimrod?''

"The Magic Loom wove a blue and gold tabard for the House of Erme. Shimrod was destroyed and the Ermes ruled until King Roble was killed at the Battle of Zemail. The Blue and Gold Tabard was lost under circumstances regarding which it would be folly to speculate, since the Magic Loom might or might not have woven the Scarlet and Gold which King Waldemar now wears. These of course are dangerous topics which I would not dare discuss with anyone but a fellow shipmaster. In any event, the colors you see signify the fervent reverence still felt for the Green and Gold, and also the deference duly rendered the Scarlet and Gold of King Waldemar. Your question, if at discursive length, has been answered.''

"All is clear," said Zamp, "except as to the Magic Loom.''

"If you would like to explore the depths of Bottomless Lake, you need only climb Myrmont.''

"I am curious, but not reckless," said Zamp.

"Such curiosity is natural," said Tush. "I was similarly affected when I first learned of the Magic Loom. Essentially I know nothing but rumor, to the effect that the loom is tended by nine Norns, who are fitful, hysterical women, either blind, dumb or deaf from birth. When one dies she selects her successor and announces her choice by means of dreams, and the new Norn then takes the name of the old.''

"The Magic Loom would appear to control the destinies of Soyvanesse," Zamp suggested.

"It is not quite so simple. Still, when King Waldemar

appears, the company will give as much reverence to the tabard as to the man."

"Master Gassoon, have you heard all this?" demanded Zamp. "To win the prize we should impress and entertain the tabard rather than the man within!"

Tush held up his hand in a quick gesture of caution. "Be careful with your jokes; skewed phrases carry far in Mornune. Already we have far overstepped discretion, and here now is King Waldemar. You must rise, and stand in the ritual posture—knees bent, head bowed, arms behind your back: so. Silence now; Waldemar is notorious for his impatience."

In dead silence King Waldemar entered the chamber: a man of medium stature, somewhat plump, his round, pale face surrounded by precise ringlets of moist black hair. He paused at the back of the chamber and scanned the company with restless black eyes. Zamp surreptitiously studied the tabard he wore over a jumper of rich red cloth: a garment of heavy black silk embroidered with starbursts of red and gold.

King Waldemar murmured over his shoulder to the noblemen who accompanied him, then advanced down the aisle and seated himself upon the throne which had been placed for him at the center of the front row. A respectful moment later the remainder of the audience resumed their own seats.

The lights in the chamber dimmed; through the curtains stepped a tall, slender man in amber robes with a long, glossy, amber beard. He bowed to the audience and spoke in a soft clear voice:

"For the pleasure and approval of the most gracious King Waldemar, and the noble citizens of Soyvanesse, we have chosen to celebrate a cycle of tales from the second book of the Rhiatic Myth. Our symbology follows the precepts of Phrygius Maestor; our music operates in the Fourth Mode, as many among you will recognize. Listen then to the First Chord, which orders the inchoate!'' He waved his hand; from an unseen source came a whisper of sound, waxing to a shivering gorgeous tone of many parts. The curtains drew back to reveal a landscape of colossal ruins illuminated by three suns: purple, pale green and white. From the ruins sprang, one by one, a company of beautiful men and women, clad only in white dust and violet breechclouts. To the music of lutes, tambourines and oboes, they performed a stiff, stately ballet. The clang of a gong: down swooped green-scaled half-human beings with cockatrice heads to smite the men and women to the ground and tear out their tongues. The green creatures performed a strutting pavane of triumph, which became a frenzied stamping dance, during which the suns changed color to red, dark orange and black. A thin clangor of bells interrupted the music; a rain of white sparks fell, shriveling the creatures and exploding them in puffs of vapor. The men and women reappeared, carrying black disks as tall as themselves, with which they performed a set of revolutions. The light began to grow dim; the dancers brought their disks together and superimposed them, disappearing behind, until a single black disk occupied the center of the stage. It turned sideways; all behind had disappeared just as the stage became dark.

The second phase of the cycle occurred in a bleak plain, with the ruins of the first scene upon the distant horizon. To a throbbing spurting music which seemed only barely under control an epicene creature performed a writhing contortion. As it threw back its arms in an evocation of the heavens, a shaft of intense white light streaming with tinsel strands struck down upon the creature, forcing it to the ground where it was absorbed into the soil. A black and green plant sprouted and grew and put forth a white flower. A second shaft of light struck into the flower which, so fertilized, closed into a pod. Silence: heavy, suspenseful seconds: then a faint crystalline tinkling sound. The pod fell apart to reveal a golden-skinned nymph. She stood still and stiff, arms at her sides. A fanfare: from the left came a black hero, from the right a red hero, wearing only kirtles and magnificent helmets. They fought with swords and the black hero triumphed. He advanced to claim the golden nymph. He touched her: the stage exploded to an effulgence of sparks; the black hero shivered and toppled dead. In joy the nymph pirouetted, whirling faster and faster; the music keened and wailed and the stage went black.

In the final phase the dancers constructed a fane of three pillars and an altar, then formed an armature upon which they molded black clay, to produce a monstrous face. Others brought torches and applied fire to the face, which thereupon opened its mouth and bawled in pain. The eyes opened, glared right and left, while those who had built the temple waved their torches and jerked to a convulsive music. The image began to chant in a harsh voice: first a babble of nonsense; then, as if gaining understanding, it produced a song increasingly melodious until at last, by the force of its music, it compelled the dancers, urging them to its impulses, while the stage grew lurid and smoky, and the dancers sweated and twitched. The image uttered a great pulsing cry, and the dancers fell together in a heap. Flames burnt on the altar and the image became silent.

The curtain fell; the slender man in the amber silks appeared and bowed gravely. "Thank you for your presence. This has been our statement and we hope that you have been affected." He bowed again.

King Waldemar, his face a mask, arose, and the

entire audience arose and stood in the formal posture of respect as Waldemar departed the chamber.

Roald Tush turned to Zamp: "What do you think?"

"Extremely powerful, most ingenious," muttered Zamp.

Gassoon said in a bleak voice: "I found the matter somewhat dense, even overportentous."

Tush laughed. "The *Voyuz* is noted for its remarkable effects. And regardless of our personal opinions, we all must ask ourselves: did Waldemar like it? He is said to prefer prettier stuff, and he might not have enjoyed all the sparks and explosions and screams so close in his face. In due course we shall know. Well then—tomorrow night to Lulu Chalu's *Star-wisp*, then to my ship, the *Perfumed Oliolus*, for one of my own poor specialties. . . . Your turn is sixth and last? No disadvantage, I should think. What type of presentation will you offer?"

"A classic drama of ancient Earth,' said Zamp. "It is said to have artistic merit."

"Ha ha! Don't count on oversubtlety from Waldemar! He searches too anxiously for signs of sedition. Who knows what colors the Magic Loom weaves at this moment?"

The *Star-wisp*'s presentation was no less notable for imaginative structure, technical virtuosity and assiduous attention to detail than that of the *Voyuz*. Again the theme, for Zamp at least, was lost, or at best dimly sensed, in the welter of fantastic spectacle. A bearded skald and his harp sang to a bevy of maidens in the hall of an olden castle. From his instrument fumes of dream-smoke billowed and parted to illustrate episodes from his ballad. In the first scene a band of giants, actually men on stilts, executed an eccentric dance, among an orchard of trees with gray and green leaves. Children in the guise of birds sang in the branches and devoured golden fruit.

Another episode began with a pair of children, idly musing, given the free latitude of their wishes by a magic being. The children wished for riches and palaces, and fleet-footed steeds; they wished for strength and power and wisdom. They began to vie with each other and each began to dread the other's force; the two ended as a pair of demons battling among a group of orbiting worlds, which they seized and hurled at each other. The white demon seized the black demon and thrust his head into a sun. . . . Mists obscured the scene and again the two children lay in the sunlit meadow. They rose to their feet, looked at each other in consternation; while a curtain of shimmering gray-violet gauze dropped in front of them. On the substage below the skald sang on to his earnest young audience.

Gassoon and Zamp returned to *Miraldra's Enchantment* in disconsolate silence. They went to Gassoon's office for a dram of spirits and for a period discussed the *Star-wisp*'s presentation. Gassoon grumbled about the technical polish which distinguished the shows aboard both the *Voyuz* and the *Star-wisp*. "In my opinion such fanatic attention to detail denotes an almost ignoble myopia, an unconcern for larger concepts. Except—," Gassoon's voice trailed off.

Zamp sighed. "I fear that our production may suffer in comparison. Our sets are shabby, our costumes makeshift. The truth of the matter is that we have tried to succeed on the cheap. We have achieved only the slipshod."

Gassoon, normally abstemious, emptied his glass and poured another dram. "We have no apologies to make," he stated in a hollow voice. "Our production explores the ultimates of human experience; we have dealt faithfully with a most difficult subject. What if our sets are other than sumptuous, our costumes unconvincing? We are artists, not pedants!''

Zamp said thoughtfully, ''King Waldemar is by no means a pedant, but still less an artist, or so I suspect.''

Gassoon glared across the table with cold dislike. ''Apollon Zamp, I hold you responsible for the flaws! You have arranged matters so that I am a laughingstock aboard my own ship!''

Zamp held up his hand. ''Please be calm, Master Gassoon. We are not defeated yet.''

''I will hear no more! Be so good as to leave my office!''

Instead of returning to his quarters, Zamp went to Damsel Blanche-Aster's cabin and tapped on the door. Her voice came from within. ''Who is it?''

''Apollon Zamp.''

The door opened; Damsel Blanche-Aster looked forth. ''What do you want at this late hour?''

''I am worried for your health. I have hardly seen you for days.''

''I am entirely well, thank you.''

''Do you intend to go ashore to pursue your business —whatever it may be?''

''There is no great hurry. I will do what needs to be done after our performance. Goodnight, Master Zamp.'' The door closed.

Zamp grimaced and turned away. At the tavern across the esplanade he took a solitary glass of wine and listened to the gossip of the docks. The presentation of the *Star-wisp* was generally considered to exceed that of the *Voyuz*, but in everyone's opinion the direction of King Waldemar's judgment was unpredictable.

On the following evening Gassoon at first decided to

remain aboard *Miraldra's Enchantment*, then at the last moment changed his mind and accompanied Zamp to the *Perfumed Oliolus*.

King Waldemar arrived precisely on the hour. He might have used a mask for a face, Zamp reflected; never had his expression altered. As always, he wore the red and gold tabard, the repository of his royal *mana*.

Roald Tush's presentation was different in both mood and form from either of the previous two, and culminated with a heart-stopping battle between children in red beetle-coats and an army of pallid dwarfs prickling with black horns like sea urchins. The children had no taste for the battle, but discipline was maintained by ferocious leaders in garments of black and white leather who strode back and forth, urging the shrieking cravens forward with whips.

On the fourth evening Zamp and Gassoon went aboard the enormous *Dellora*. Before the performance one of King Waldemar's heralds made a most dampening announcement to the effect that King Waldemar, being dissatisfied with those entertainments rendered to date, had added a proviso to the terms of the contest. The winner, as before, would be rewarded, but the company which in King Waldemar's opinion had offered the poorest spectacle would be adjudged guilty of perpetrating an insolence. The penalties were severe: the shipmaster must pay a fine equal to one-tenth the value of his ship; each member of the company, stripped naked, would receive five vigorous strokes of the rattan; the noses of all would be tattooed pale blue.

Whether by reason of the threat or through innate excellence the company of the *Dellora* produced a set of amazing spectacles, both unusual and recondite. A company of punchinellos performed prodigious feats of buffoonery; a company of ecstatically beautiful dancers created a living kaleidoscope, and five magicians displayed a set of illusions which left Zamp in a state of baffled amazement. At the finale a tall screen extended across the stage. Through holes peered faces, some pallid and dreary, some comatose, some smirking, rolling their eyes and wagging their tongues back and forth. Balls of black fluff moved up and down and horizontally across the screen, brushing the faces which thereupon moaned mournful musical tones. From the floor of the stage a black curtain rose; as each face became covered it performed a hideous grimace of despair, then became blank.

Zamp and Gassoon trudged slowly back to *Miraldra's Enchantment*, each busy with his own speculations. Gassoon managed an overloud laugh. "It is entirely possible that our pessimism is unfounded. Our production, if nothing else, projects an elemental vitality, and after all, why must we minimize the noble poetry, the passion and intensity of our vehicle? I believe that we will win the competition after all! Still we must be vigilant; our worst pitfall is bathos. I am dissatisfied with my costume, for instance. Duncan is kingly, ponderous, profound; a white and blue surcoat conveys an overtone of frivolity. In your turn, you must pitch your voice to a deeper resonance, so that, in the soliloquies, your words can be heard without your seeming to shout out across the audience. I also suggest that the tender caresses between Lord and Lady Macbeth be minimized; we are not celebrating their nuptials in this drama."

"I will do my best, most certainly," said Zamp with dignity.

On the fifth evening the company of the *Empyrean Wanderer* presented a vivacious pageant of farce and frivolity. Beautiful maidens bounded from springboard to springboard high above the stage carrying hoops of colored lights; to the left of the stage clowns tried to resuscitate four corpses; to the right a timid apprentice sought to shoe a demoniac black horse. A great egg burst open; naked children ran forth trailing colored streamers; a troupe of twenty men and women, dressed to represent various racial types, sang satirical songs relative to each other's habits. The clowns finally succeeded in their effort; the corpses arose, explained their theories of existence, capered with the clowns, sang comic ballads and jigged offstage. In the finale a web of pyrotechnics lit the stage; two men in white tights shot from cannons met in the air above mid-stage, clasped each other and swung to safety on a trapeze; satyrs chased the maidens back and forth; the orchestra all the while playing merry quicksteps.

Zamp, peering across the audience, saw King Waldemar's face soften into a smile, and he muttered an approving comment to one of his attendants.

On the sixth evening Apollon Zamp and his company would present before King Waldemar and the nobility of Mornune the tragic drama *Macbeth* aboard *Miraldra's Enchantment*.

During the day tension pressed heavy upon the ship. Zamp reviewed the sets, ordered alterations and improvements, rearranged the lighting. Gassoon strode back and forth with white hair askew, making strange gestures, then went into his museum and rummaged about in hope of finding regal adjuncts to his costume. Damsel Blanche-Aster showed no interest in the performance. She came up to the quarterdeck and watched the preparations with an expression of detachment. Gassoon joined her and made a gesture of revulsion toward Zamp. "This fiasco is all his doing! Now we are threatened with fines, confiscation, humiliation and pain! Do you consider this a sensible adventure for persons such as you and me? We will detach ourselves from this idiotic charade on this instant and sail back down the placid Vissel, and at last we will live the life we have planned!''

Damsel Blanche-Aster shook her head. ''You would not be allowed to withdraw from the competition. Who knows? Perhaps King Waldemar will be favorably impressed.''

''If only I had resisted the arguments of that charlatan Zamp!'' groaned Gassoon and took himself off to his museum.

By mid-afternoon Zamp had worked himself into a state of lethargy. He no longer doubted the outcome of the evening's program; it was simply inconceivable that his troupe, with its eccentric acting, fallible memories and extraordinary music, should arouse King Waldemar's enthusiasm.

So passed the afternoon. Phaedra coasted west across a cloudless sky. The lake lay limpid, a blue patina blandly concealing the dark miles below.

The troupe took a late-afternoon meal, then went off to costume themselves. Zamp brushed the velvet of King Waldemar's throne for the tenth time, cast a despairing glance around the weather-beaten deck, and himself went off to change into costume.

The sun dropped beyond the hills. Daylight failed and the lights of Mornune twinkled up the Myrmont slopes. Aboard *Miraldra's Enchantment* cressets flared, and presently the first members of the audience sauntered up the gangplank and took their places. Zamp watched through a peephole, and thought that they stared in amusement at the far from splendid appurtenances of the ship.

The audience was in place. Backstage, tension almost crackled. Damsel Blanche-Aster stood to the side, wearing a gray cape against the evening chill. Gassoon still made last-minute adjustments with his costume and Zamp sent a petulant call into his dressing room urging him to haste. "King Waldemar approaches along the esplanade now!"

"No matter," said Gassoon. "There is ample time; my entrance is not immediate! What of the witches?"

"They are at hand."

"Lady Macbeth?"

"Ready."

"Yourself?"

"Ready."

"Then there is no difficulty. The orchestra can play a double overture, if necessary."

"Bah," muttered Zamp. "Well, we will do what we can."

King Waldemar boarded the ship and was conducted to his place. Zamp, his costume shrouded in a black cloak, waited a polite moment, then stepped forth upon the stage.

"Tonight, for the pleasure of King Waldemar and his distinguished fellowship, we evoke a presence from the remote past. *Macbeth* is a legend of medieval Earth; an authentic text somehow found its way to Coble on Surmise Bay and into the wonderful collection of Throdorus Gassoon. When we learned of King Waldemar's festival, we knew that nothing would serve but a recreation of this archaic masterpiece!

"Without further ado, we take you across time and space to a 'desert place,' somewhere in Scotland, where three bearded witches contrive the evil which propels the entire drama." Zamp bowed and stepped backstage.

The curtain drew back with a squeak and a rustle.

* * *

First Witch: When shall we three meet again,
                 In thunder, lightning or in rain?
Second Witch: When the hurly-burly's done . . .

Watching through the peephole, Zamp was pleased to note that at the very least King Waldemar's attention had been captured. He remembered the dilatory Gassoon. Still in his dressing room? But no: Gassoon had come forth, cloaked, booted and cowled, his regality symbolized by a curious old many-pronged headpiece of wood and iron, and Zamp was forced to admit that Gassoon in all aspects projected royal dignity.

Duncan: What bloody man is that? He can report,
          as seemth by his plight, of the revolt
          The newest state.
Malcolm: This is the sergeant . . .

Scene Two went off satisfactorily, thought Zamp. Now Scene Three and again the witches, on "a heath near Forres."

First Witch: Where has thou been, sister?
Second Witch: Killing swine.
Third Witch: Sister, where thou?
First Witch: A sailor's wife . . .

Zamp, as Macbeth, came on stage, with Banquo. The two heard the prophesies and received news from Ross and Angus.

Now down with the curtain and away to Scene Three-and-a-half, that scene which Zamp had interpolated, both in accordance with his theories of mood-augmentation, and the better to display Damsel Blanche-Aster's cool and exquisite beauty.

The sets shifted; the stage became a formal garden at Glamis Castle. The curtain lifted, to reveal Lady Macbeth at a table inscribing a letter with a quill pen. As Zamp had constructed the scene, she would read phrases from the letter encouraging Macbeth in his ambitions; but now Damsel Blanche-Aster saw fit to alter the scene. As soon as the curtain had drawn fully aside, she rose to her feet, doffed her cloak and moved to the front of the stage to stand full in the footlights, and all could see that Damsel Blanche-Aster wore a blue and gold tabard similar to that red and gold garment worn by King Waldemar. From the audience came a gutsy exhalation of shock and wonder.

Damsel Blanche-Aster said, "I wear the Blue and Gold; I received it from my father, and you all know my identity. There is no force in the Scarlet and Gold. Who recognizes the Blue and Gold and the House of Erme?"

King Waldemar had jumped to his feet, a curious uncertain expression on his face. Zamp stood frozen in the wings. How could he have ever thought the noblemen of Mornune cold and remote? Eyes glittered, jaws clenched to draw back the mouths into tight, tense grins. In all quarters there was slow motion converging upon Waldemar, who darted glances from side to side. Suddenly he turned and started for the gangplank.

Damsel Blanche-Aster said in a clear voice, "Lord Haze, Lord Brouwe, Lord Valicour: take the person of Waldemar the murderer into your control. Convey him out upon the deep lake and there do what must be done."

Three noblemen bowed and came forward. They took the dazed Waldemar by the arms and led him away.

Damsel Blanche-Aster stood stiff and cold. Gassoon, removing his cloak for the next scene, became aware of the interruption. He peered out through the wings, and noticed that for some remarkable reason—perhaps a coarse comment from the audience—Damsel Blanche-Aster had faltered in her performance. He rushed forth in reckless fury, to glare across the footlights. "I beg all of you to courtesy! Our performance has only just begun!" He turned to Damsel Blanche-Aster. "Please, my dear, continue with your scene!"

Damsel Blanche-Aster stared at him first with cold annoyance, then incredulous eyes and a mouth which gaped more loosely than had Waldemar's. From the audience came a strange wail of awe and dread for the presence of the uncanny. Gassoon's attention however was riveted upon Damsel Blanche-Aster. Gone was her self-possession, she seemed no more than a frightened girl. Gassoon cried out: "What is the matter? Why do you look at me so?"

Damsel Blanche-Aster pointed a shaking finger at him. "You wear the fabled Green and Gold—the Green and Gold Tabard! Where did you get it?"

Gassoon looked down slack-jawed at the brittle old garment which, so he had hoped, might invest Duncan with something of that kingly style he had observed in Waldemar. "From my collection of antique garments."

Damsel Blanche-Aster numbly removed the Blue and Gold. "The warp of the Magic Loom leads not to me. You are King of Soyvanesse and Emperor of Fay."

Gassoon struggled for words. "I am reluctant to make such claims. . . . I am Throdorus Gassoon."

"Your will is nothing. The Magic Loom has woven this destiny for you, and it is incontrovertible. This is the miracle Soyvanesse has hoped for; you must accept both the glory and the responsibility."

Gassoon pulled doubtfully at his long white nose. "Most remarkable indeed. Zamp, have you heard all this?"

"Yes," said Zamp. "I've heard and seen it all. What of our performance? Shall we continue? It seems that now you must sit in judgment."

"I have already made up my mind," declared Gassoon in sudden exaltation. "The grand prize goes to *Miraldra's Enchantment* and its magnificent troupe! I also decree munificent second prizes for the talented troupes of the *Voyuz*, the *Star-wisp*, the *Perfumed Oliolus*, the *Dellora* and the *Empyrian Wanderer*. All performances were excellent; the penalty suggested by the late King Waldemar is nullified. I invite all present to the royal palace where we will celebrate this remarkable event, and now, while the idea is fresh in my mind, I appoint, designate and select Princess Blanche-Aster to be my consort, my adored and intimate companion, a condition she and I have long anticipated and which tonight we will consecrate. What did you say, Master Zamp?"

"Nothing of consequence, Master Gassoon."

"Well then, be so good as to show more elation for these happy circumstances!"

"I will indeed."

"Good! Excellent, in fact! Bring forth Garth Ashgale and his miserable troupe! I hereby remit their indentures! Bring forth Baron Banoury and his cutthroats and give them into custody! They must answer for their crimes. As for you, Apollon Zamp, I hereby forgive you a long score of offenses, petty impertinences and frauds. In fact, I invest you with full title to *Miraldra's Enchantment* and all its appurtenances, in fee simple and perpetual. I will no longer have need for such a vessel."

Zamp bowed. "I thank you most gratefully, King Throdorus."

"Aha!" cried Gassoon. "Marvelous indeed are the ways of the Magic Loom! So now—all to the royal palace!"

Chapter 15

Many adversities had ingrained in Zamp the conviction that the time to leave was when conditions were auspicious. After three days of festivity he decided to depart Mornune and make his way south along the Vissel. Gassoon, a most indulgent monarch, granted him leave to do as he wished. "Still, why not remain at Mornune? As a courtesy due an old crony, I will appoint you a Grandee of the Realm, and settle upon you an appropriate estate: honors which in fact you already have earned, in line with Waldemar's proclamation."

Zamp was not to be dissuaded. "As you know, I am three parts wandering minstrel to one part aristocrat. The river winds blow in my blood! If you wish, you may grant me an equivalence of iron, so that I may construct the grandest boat yet seen on the Vissel, or the Cynthiana, or elsewhere!"

Gassoon attempted an indulgent gesture, but restrained the swing of his arm. The Green and Gold Tabard constricted his shoulders, and forced him to careful and controlled motions lest he burst the brittle fabric. The Princess Blanche-Aster, on a couch of carved jade, sat blank-faced, like a porcelain doll. "As you wish, but you must promise to bring your magnificent new show-

boat to Mornune on its maiden voyage to regale us with
your fancies and fantasies.''

"I will certainly do so," declared Zamp.

Gassoon summoned an equerry. "Convey at once
twenty ingots of black iron to Master Zamp's authority
aboard *Miraldra's Enchantment*."

Zamp bowed once to Gassoon and again to Princess
Blanche-Aster, who returned an abstracted nod. Zamp
thought she seemed dull and bloodless. Her green silk
gown was embroidered with pearls and black iron beads;
her blonde hair had been worked into an elaborate
confection of curls and coils. Was it for this that she
had returned to Mornune? "Without further formality,"
said Zamp, "I will take my leave."

"May fair winds fill your sails."

At the portal Zamp turned and gave a final salute.
Gassoon stood as before, tall and gaunt, wild white hair
tufted through his iron crown, bony wrists protruding
from the fabulous tabard.

Returning to *Miraldra's Enchantment*, Zamp certified
the quality of the twenty ingots, to the total of two
hundred pounds. Assured that all his personnel were
aboard, he gave orders to cast off lines, and make all
sail south.

Bottomless Lake lay flat as a mirror; the sails hung
limp. Zamp ordered the stern wheel down, the bullocks
and Garth Ashgale's crew to the capstan. Garth Ashgale
set up an outcry. "Our indentures have been lifted; we
are now free men and need not toil at the capstan!''

"You are free men indeed," said Zamp, "but you
must earn your way back to Coble, which means the
capstan. If you prefer to remain at Mornune, feel free to
swim ashore!''

Grumbling and muttering, Garth Ashgale led his troupe
to the capstans.

The showboat churned across the lake. After an hour, Zamp raised the stern wheel and drifted silently south on what vagrant airs struck the sails.

At noon on the following day, the vessel passed through the Mandaman Gate and, riding the current, swept past Banoury Castle without challenge. To either side spread the Tinsitala Steppe; ahead stretched the Vissel.

The south monsoon had definitely died; winds were captious and fickle, blowing first one way, then another. Zamp was in no hurry. An hour in the morning and an hour in the afternoon he turned his stern wheel to provide exercise both for the bullocks and for Garth Ashgale; otherwise he was content to float on the current, while he drew up specifications for his wonderful new vessel. He would command the rarest woods, the most elaborate carving, the best Lanteen glass! There would be luxurious quarters for troupe and crew alike, and for himself a great stern cabin with mullioned casements looking aft down the wake. He would specify colonnaded upper decks like those which graced the *Voyur*, a stage as ingenious as that of the *Dellora*, banks of folding seats like those of the *Empyrean Wanderer*. The deck would be hinged to slide the audience overboard, and also equipped with a drop-section to precipitate troublemakers into a cargo net: both systems had proved their worth. Stern wheel? Side wheels? Propellers? Zamp delayed decision. His repertory? Classical dramas from antique Earth? Ha ha! And Zamp, leaning back in his chair, watched the clouds drift across the wide Big Planet sky.

On the fourth day after passing through the Mandaman Gate Zamp's attention was attracted by a wildly galloping horseman on the east bank of the river. The horseman, drawing abreast of the ship, performed a set of urgent gesticulations: looking through the spyglass Zamp identified the man as Throdorus Gassoon.

Zamp ordered the sails backed and sent a boat to the shore. Gassoon, sagging with fatigue, his skin red and coarse from sunburn, presently joined him on the quarterdeck.

"Well then, King Throdorus," said Zamp, "this is an honor and a privilege, but I had not expected to see you so soon."

Gassoon drank down the glass of brandy proffered by Zamp. "King Throdorus no more," he croaked. "I am now as before, Throdorus Gassoon of Coble, and I have no regrets, I assure you. But what do you have on hand that I might eat? I am ravenous with hunger!"

Zamp ordered up a meal of bread, cheese, meat and preserved leeks; as Gassoon ate, he related the circumstances which had brought him back to the showboat. The tale, in essence, was succinct. The Green and Gold Tabard, brittle with age and subjected to the strain of fitting Gassoon's ill-proportioned form, had suddenly disintegrated into shreds. Gassoon immediately calculated that if possession of the tabard transformed him from an uncouth down-river boatman to King of Soyvanesse, then the lack of the same tabard must perform an equivalent metamorphosis in reverse.

He had confided nothing to the Princess Blanche-Aster. "In all honesty I must report that while her conduct was most dutiful and correct, I detected a lack of enthusiasm in certain aspects of our relationship. I am inclined to suspect that our very real mutuality was of the spirit, rather than the physical. To be totally candid—well, let me say only that I kept my own counsel in regard to the tabard. To make a long story short, I decided to rejoin my good comrade Apollon Zamp, in the hope that the old association held firm."

Zamp poured himself a dram of brandy. "The association is firm. The boat is once more yours and the iron you were generous enough to bestow shall be divided between us. There is ample wealth for the two of us."

Gassoon raised his finger in a sly gesture. "I will keep my vessel; it is once more the *Universal Pancomium*; and you shall keep the iron." He kicked the saddlebags on the deck beside him. "Here are diamonds, rubies and emeralds, as well as great black opals set in iron. Our wealth is by no means disproportionate."

Zamp poured brandy into both glasses. "The association has been profitable, Throdorus!"

"Profitable, instructive and edifying."

The two men drank, then turned to look north up the Vissel at the far shadow of the Mandaman Palisades. At this moment a breeze veering down from the equatorial trades filled the sails. With foam at the bow and a gurgle to the wake, the ship surged south down the Vissel toward far Coble.

THE BEST IN SCIENCE FICTION

☐	54989-9	STARFIRE by Paul Preuss	$3.95
☐	54990-2		Canada $4.95
☐	54281-9	DIVINE ENDURANCE by Gwyneth Jones	$3.95
☐	54282-7		Canada $4.95
☐	55696-8	THE LANGUAGES OF PAO by Jack Vance	$3.95
☐	55697-6		Canada $4.95
☐	54892-2	THE THIRTEENTH MAJESTRAL by Hayford Peirce	$3.95
☐	54893-0		Canada $4.95
☐	55425-6	THE CRYSTAL EMPIRE by L. Neil Smith	$4.50
☐	55426-4		Canada $5.50
☐	53133-7	THE EDGE OF TOMORROW by Isaac Asimov	$3.95
☐	53134-5		Canada $4.95
☐	55800-6	FIRECHILD by Jack Williamson	$3.95
☐	55801-4		Canada $4.95
☐	54592-3	TERRY'S UNIVERSE ed. by Beth Meacham	$3.50
☐	54593-1		Canada $4.50
☐	53355-0	ENDER'S GAME by Orson Scott Card	$3.95
☐	53356-9		Canada $4.95
☐	55413-2	HERITAGE OF FLIGHT by Susan Shwartz	$3.95
☐	55414-0		Canada $4.95

Buy them at your local bookstore or use this handy coupon:
Clip and mail this page with your order.

Publishers Book and Audio Mailing Service
P.O. Box 120159, Staten Island, NY 10312-0004

Please send me the book(s) I have checked above. I am enclosing $_____
(please add $1.25 for the first book, and $.25 for each additional book to
cover postage and handling. Send check or money order only—no CODs.)

Name_____

Address_____

City_____State/Zip_____

Please allow six weeks for delivery. Prices subject to change without notice.